GIFT HORSE

GIFT
HORSE

by

JAMES L. SUMMERS

THE WESTMINSTER PRESS
Philadelphia

J

LIBRARY OF CONGRESS CATALOG CARD NO. 61–5564

PRINTED IN THE UNITED STATES OF AMERICA

For
Cathy Davis

GIFT HORSE

1:

ALAN WHITLOCK emerged into the sunburned patio and stood at the sliding glass door. Aunt Ava and his mother were still talking.

"The very idea! " Aunt Ava's voice carried to him. " An automobile for that half-grown boy, Alice? Why, I do declare, haven't you and Tom read those surveys about how cars ruin a boy's grade average and dominate his life, not to mention the accidents! Don't worry about college; he'll probably drop out of high school, and — "

"Yak — yak — yak! " Alan whispered wearily. " That's all she does."

He slid the door closed. Out here he was alone — until they yelled at him to do some stupid deed; women, especially aunts and mothers, were loaded with mad whims.

He glanced across the back lawn into the uncultivated open yard that sloped gently upward toward the approaches of Oak Hill. Briefly, he debated between holing up in the garage or seeking open seclusion among the calm oaks. The safest plan would be to duck out completely to Wigwam's house, or maybe Newton's, but his mother had already told him to hang around here — in readiness, sort of. Later on, the whole family was going to the Surfrider Inn so that Aunt Ava, who came from Oklahoma, got this genuine shore dinner stuffed down her.

For the moment at least he was free; he could — Alan Whitlock stiffened in chill terror. There was something

7

slithering across his bare ankles, some slick and creepy living object like a warm snake! He stared down in horror. Sure enough, there it was.

"Yap! Yap!" said this hot rattlesnake.

Alan's eyes narrowed in repugnant recognition. It wasn't a rattler; it was King Sinaloa Aztec II, wearing his crazy little turtle-neck dog sweater in the hundred-degree heat. A guy might know it would be that dog instead of some kindly reptile.

His voice was muted to a barely audible growl, filled with the menace of steamy jungles. "You shut up," Alan snarled softly. "You get out of here: go back where you came from!"

The King weighed about a pound and a half. He looked somewhat like a miniature deer, with big erect ears and large, protruding brown eyes swimming in liquid — as if he were about to bawl over the sorrow a good little Chihuahua had to endure.

The animal recognized Alan's hard tone and bounced away a few mincing steps, but, though prudent, The King was far from a coward. Given the right provocation, that dog would argue with a tiger, probably. "Yap!" repeated The King; he followed this positive admonition with a series of high-pitched, Spanish-type sounds.

Alan's tone changed instantly. "Don't do that," he pleaded. "Try to keep quiet a while, please." His whisper, though hoarse, was filled with the sort of sound dog logic a genuine dog could readily understand.

King Sinaloa Aztec II did not understand. He wagged his thin, naked tail like a hummingbird's wing and frisked around just out of reach, meanwhile screaming his tiny hysteria.

Alan groaned aloud. This racket meant that his sister, Dorothea, would be out here any second. She had been mistress of King Aztec II ever since Aunt Ava had arrived so long ago with about seven suitcases and a wicker basket. For the two whole days, it had made Alan shudder just to

8

think about how cute Dorothea thought that dog was in his little velveteen basket bed. It gave a fairly gruesome impression of his kid sister's intelligence, and boded ill besides.

Sure enough, the sliding door zipped open and the flame of next year's ninth grade at Lamagra High blew out. "King!" Dorothea shrieked. "Oh-h!" spotting that half-dog, "did anyone hurt ums?"

"Of course not —" Alan began, while King Sinaloa danced forward in a frenzy of insane recognition and jumped into the girl's outstretched arms.

"Oo-h-h!" Dorothea squealed again. "Him's all right, isn't hims?" meanwhile examining the wriggling creature for busted backbones and stuff. "Oh-h-h, I'm so glad. So-o-o glad!"

For one unbearable flash Alan allowed himself to view the sight his sister and her dog from outer space created in an otherwise fairly decent June landscape. In moments of bleak honesty, he had to admit that Dorothea was a mighty pretty little kid with greenish eyes and sun-streaked blond hair. She had nice, even teeth and a good bite besides, plus a lot of misdirected energy that made her too smart in school for anyone's good. It showed a person how important was the mind. Dorothea's mind wasn't too stable.

"Why did you do it?" she now demanded, flinging around toward him with The King cuddled deep. "I begged you not to let him out."

It was brain-buzz. Alan shut his eyes. "I didn't let him out."

"He's out, isn't he?" declared Dorothea, using woman's logic. "You just tell me how, if you didn't let him out. Nobody else went —"

Alan sighed and blew out his cheeks by reflex action. "You don't *let* a thing like that out, 'Thea. It crawls under stuff like doors, and — it —"

"Stop talking like that about my dog," Dorothea sniffed,

9

" or I'll — " A wicked light sprang into her elfish eyes. " I'll tell Aunt Ava — "

" Go ahead," he babbled recklessly. " Tell her; tell your uncles. Call up the humane society, and — "

Her tone was dangerous. " I will tell Aunt Ava, if you don't promise never to let King out again."

" I promise," he said.

" Open your eyes and say it. Say, ' I promise I won't let King out ever again.' And uncross your fingers behind your back."

A flicker of rebellion came into the slave's icy heart. " King? " he asked in genuine curiosity. " You really going to call him that? " He grinned. " Call him Thing, why don't you. It rhymes."

" Alan Whitlock! You stop that. You open your eyes and promise or I'll tell Aunt Ava you're calling her gift dog a *thing*. Then you'll see."

Well, it showed how a bad influence could come into the home and ruin everything, Alan realized. Usually, Dorothea was a fairly neat sister and his parents were easy to live with. The family had been planning a short trip to Yosemite this week and he'd actually looked forward to it. Then Aunt Ava's telegram had come.

He opened his gray eyes and stared with compassion upon Dorothea, who was only a child after all, but spoiled. " Honestly, I didn't purposely let out that — I mean, your precious dog," he told her in a sincere, melancholy voice, " and I won't do it again, unless — Well, he just comes out by himself when somebody opens the door, 'Thea. I didn't see him do it; who could? "

His sister was still spoiled. " All right," she told him imperiously and went into the house with the dog draped over her shoulder so that Alan had the misfortune to meet the little beast's eyes. King Aztec II was leering back at him through a vista in Dorothea's hair. It was an apparition too ghastly for the ordinary human eyeball.

" Agh! " he had to exclaim. " Agh! "

10

After that, he stood still for a moment, bowed with this new weight of despair added to the usual crushing burden. He noticed the regular herd of supersparrows jabbing their beaks this way and that out in the yard. Here and there weeds grew and gophers gnawed rose roots and prize tubers. A sort of ominously ticking silence permeated everything for a full minute until another jet from Reno or Vandenberg went over and busted the sound barrier again.

It was life in Lamagra; a guy had to get adjusted to it or else.

His feet began to plod him forward — large, heavy, unreliable feet put together with weak rubber bands, evidently. They dragged him to the shade of the garage, where the day's heat had intensified the smell garden tools gave off to the one guy who had to push them around. It wasn't unpleasant — if you happened to like essence of lawn mower.

Facing the wall, he leaned against the doorjamb, one tall, tired youth with almost too much trouble to lug around any further. Alan was thin, and weak in looks, as he knew himself from one more scathing self-appraisal this morning. Every day he had to fight off a recurring sense of standing outside his own personality and evaluating Alan Whitlock with the narrow, hard eyes of a critical stranger. Truthfully, he doubted that a person so weak and no-good was likely to live beyond about seventeen. That left him just a few weeks more than a year to go in life.

Once again he pictured them bending over the pitiful *corpus delicti* stretched out there on the spot where it had dropped dead beside the family trash bins. They were wringing skinny paws of grief.

"Why did you listen to Aunt Ava?" his fine old father would be moaning. "We could at least have let him own a car even though it did cut down a little on the crazy grade average. After all, I did teach him to drive." One thin ray of comfort was that he had a good dad.

11

He pushed the idea out of his mind because it would just be a lot of trouble and expense for the family; besides, he was probably too weak even to drop dead. He'd have to go on despite everything including Aunt Ava and her ideas about cars, although it meant it would be a lot longer than a year before his folks let him have some transportation. By that time it would be too late, but his parents — especially his mother — were easily influenced by wagging tongues. Aunt Ava's could really wag.

Alan lifted the garage door and limped inside. He sat down on a sawhorse at the far end. Here his father had set up a workshop with some power tools and the lapidary outfit. Whenever Tom Whitlock got some time off from being manager of the Lamagra Guarantee Loan Association he liked to come out to this refuge and polish a few stones. He was a rock hound. Now that a son thought it over, though, his dad hadn't polished a rock for a couple of years and only about a half dozen all told. He'd seemed to lose interest and was probably barely able to go on too. Well, like father, like son.

Gradually Alan's head sank down until he had to cup his chin in both hands to hold it up, and wouldn't a guy know it? His brain began to think despite everything a person did to prevent that.

" Becky! " he groaned.

Speaking her cherished name that way revived love's eternal agony — although he tried to fight it off. No use; there she was again: Becky Linnell, the neatest girl in next year's junior class and the whole world.

Last semester in algebra he'd made real progress in winning her adoration. The inevitable day had come when she'd turned around to where he sat just behind her and flashed that blazing smile. Becky had hair the color of a red hawk's wing — a sheeny russet with deep lights hidden in her feathers — and her eyes were blue, like fire in ice. She was all right.

Then that woman had done the wonderful and fantastic;

she'd asked him to explain the stupid assignment. Since it was the last class of the day, for a whole fifteen minutes they'd sat beside each other in this crazy togetherness while doing the little things of love. Little things like her algebra problems; the best, man.

"You're a brain, Alan," she'd breathed when he'd whipped through the final equation. "Thanks, endlessly."

Then right away he'd begun to lose her, which was to be expected with his luck. Her father, Mr. J. T. Linnell, who was manager of the American Bank, bought her a horse and she'd joined the Pony Belles, which was the girls' junior version of the Cow Wranglettes, the women's auxiliary of the Lamagra Mounted Sheriff's Posse.

From then on Becky had changed. She'd become obsessed with the same horse madness of other freshman and sophomore girls who happened to be Pony Belles. She began hanging around Marcia James and Luella Larson, who were regular latigo queens of bit and saddle, as anyone could plainly see. A girl with Becky's sharp brain power should have been able to recognize the danger merely by looking at Marcia. The disease had got her to the point where she even looked like a 4-H horse, prancing around, whinnying in school and on city streets until a guy felt like handing her a bundle of alfalfa hay for lunch. Marcia was Chuck Newton's heart-beep and could ride like a girl-centaur, as the guy often pointed out. Well, he could have her big affection all he wanted.

So almost from the start, equines had tarnished Becky's blossoming love for Alan. And wouldn't you know that a character like Leroy Walker would move into the vacuum?

Walker's father owned the Cadillac agency and practically everything else in Lamagra. The family lived outside town on a small ranch called Los Negritos, where Mr. Walker raised Black Angus bulls as a hobby, so Leroy drove back and forth to school in his own Austin Healey Sprite. Not only that but the guy was a genuine killer with the women, being tall and rugged with a creamy manner

13

and you knew it because so did Leroy. Also, he got along fairly well with people and teachers.

Even without his opulent accouterments, Walker would be hopeless competition, but when you had to compete both with Leroy and a Sprite no weak Whitlock was likely to come up a winner.

Alan had finally accepted the fact that Becky was forever lost, but a guy couldn't hold down the wild dream that something might happen to put back the ecstatic magic in life. Maybe Becky's horse might even take a liking to a person, or — Well, there could be a lot of unforeseen angles. One thing about a Whitlock — the poor creep never gave up. Alan had learned that from listening to his dad. Mr. Whitlock hadn't given up although he'd faced odds as a youth, which made today's petty sophomore problems laughable by comparison. In those days, a son realized, youths had been fashioned from the real old-fashioned spirit. Stuff that was the true stuff, like cast iron.

He sighed. It hurt to think about how his cast-iron father had managed life in the good old days and how soft and spineless a lot of sons had turned out from the mold. Regular lumps.

He knew what a disappointment he was to everyone in the family, especially being the only male boy around to carry on the family name and strain. Sure, Uncle Gene Whitlock on his dad's side had two sons, but they were men and in the Navy. Everywhere else was nothing but a gang of girl cousins, so they looked to Alan for leadership, probably. Well, all they could do was to keep looking; he wasn't able to lead even a Chihuahua dog.

Maybe that explained Aunt Ava, who was his mother's sister, as Alan understood the improbable relationship. Perhaps his aunt figured that somebody had to take up the cudgels, as they said.

On his mother's side, the Reagans had been the rawhide pioneer stock of the Old West, Alan knew. Although the

14

blood got thinned something fierce from a Reagan marrying a Whitlock, Aunt Ava expected plenty from a guy who had even a drop in his veins. According to her, the manly brood had gotten started by Grandad Wink Reagan down there on the old Rio Grande.

Grandad Reagan was supposed to have named his kids for these counties in Texas, so Uncle Bruce, who was a professor of English Lit at San Diego State, was named for Brewster County. Uncle Errell, who carried on the legend in the insurance business, got named for Terrell County, and Uncle Val, a building contractor in West Covina, for Val Verde. Aunt Ava, who said she was named for Zavala County, claimed that if Mr. Whitlock had done the same thing, Alan's real name would be Santa Lamagra del Rio Whitlock, because Lamagra was in that county and he'd been born here.

At that, it might be better than a weak name like Alan, he mused. When the teacher would call on him in class, she'd say, "Who discovered gold in California, Santa Lamagra del Rio?" People would notice a guy with a distinctive name like that. But —

The deep, mellow throat of an engine gearing down nearby awakened the slumbering air, so that blue jays took off and even a few sparrows glanced up briefly from gorging themselves on the bounty.

Alan awoke more slowly from reverie and it wasn't until somebody yelled, "Whitlock!" right outside in the driveway that he looked up. The engine was abruptly cut off and silence swept back like a wave from the hills.

Alan's inner consciousness had recognized the voice of the machine; it was Newton's rod. Wearily, he arose to see what the guy wanted.

"Whitlock! Where are you?" the voice demanded again. A horn bayed like a bloodhound with a Western accent.

Alan hastened forward. "In here!" he said in hoarse apprehension. If Newton blew that horn once more, Aunt Ava would rush outside to see who the Lipan Apaches

15

were scalping this time. He didn't want that. Aunt Ava had already spoiled car ownership; he didn't want her to ruin last shreds of friendship.

Newton sat there tall in the bucket seat of his redesigned domestic six. He had come to Lamagra from the great little city of Weare, which, according to Chuck, was located on the Piscataqua River in New Hampshire. The town of Weare, Newton liked to point out, was bounded on the north by North Weare, and on the south by South Weare. "Folks in the granite state work out stuff by logic," he liked to say in his foreign accent.

He was going on seven feet tall and could play basketball like mad, yet Newton was the only true intellectual kid at Lamagra High. People said he'd become a beat except that nobody that blond could ever grow a real beard. He had pink skin and invisible eyebrows; right after going to the barber, his haircut was practically invisible too, which, combined with his ambitions, could scare people. He didn't want to become a professional basketball player, as everyone including the coach advised. No, Newton wanted to be a poet. "Guys," he'd say, "somebody has to take Sandburg's place. Also, Frost can't live forever. Who's going to do it?"

The idea had that sound New Hampshire logic; the only trouble was that Chuck's basketball was poetry while his real poetry was terrible. But wasn't that always the way?

Joe Nunez, who was with Newton, leaned out of the car and flashed his white smile. "Hi, Alan," he said softly. "You seen Wigwam?"

"No," Alan replied, strolling over and leaning on the rod. "Why? What's the trouble with Wigwam now?"

"Nothing," Joe chuckled. "Wondering, is all." He grinned. "When you do see him, I'll bet it'll be a surprise."

"True!" Newton agreed. "Tuttle is always a surprise; but this time he's outdone himself."

"You feeling all right?" Joe inquired with solicitude.

16

"I mean, you look worried, Whitlock. Something the matter?"

Alan shrugged. "Nothing new. My Aunt Ava's still here."

Joe Nunez shivered. "Yeah," he said with profound sympathy. "I seen her downtown yesterday and she's a real aunt. I got a few; plenty uncles too. But not many like your Aunt Ava."

Alan nodded appreciatively. Joe was sensitive to the other person's troubles, maybe because he'd had a few of his own by being the youngest of eight brothers and sisters. Still, he was older than most sophomores, mainly because he'd been flunked in the third grade by somebody named Miss Knuckleson. At that, he was better off; he owned a car — an old heavy job, which kept on running no matter what. The one bad feature of Joe's car was that it got only five miles on a gallon of some sort of petroleum product. Nunez never had enough in the tank to get back from wherever he'd gone.

"So Wigwam hasn't showed up?" Newton said. "That's funny. We should have passed him en route here."

"En route?" Alan inquired. "Did — did Wigwam's folks buy him a car? Why, he's still only fifteen, the same age. as I am."

Joe and Newton laughed together, as if they shared a good secret. "Not exactly," Chuck said, meanwhile opening the car door and extracting his long frame by languid degrees. Standing to full stature that way he made Alan, who was just under six feet, realize what it meant to go through the game of life as a midget.

"You'll see," Joe added, emerging from the other side. "Wigwam's got transportation, all right. He traded his bicycle for part of it."

As if by unspoken but common consent, the three youths began to wander aimlessly toward the front yard, scuffing the gravel in the driveway as they walked. At last they stood at the margin of the locust-shaded street, which was

17

really one of Lamagra's county roads, narrowly paved between wide dirt shoulders and winding through the Coast Range hills of the Salinas Valley.

"Hey!" exclaimed Joe, squinting his dark, heavily lashed eyes into the bright sunshine. "Isn't that — Look down there toward the creek, guys."

All stared. Then Alan made a choking sound. Approaching around the curve, which mounted upward from the creek, were three figures he knew too well by the animals they rode. Becky and her two Pony Belle chums — chestnut, blood bay, and that simpering black filly, which was the equivalent of a girl horse. Miss Moonfire, she called that creepy nag that had ruined a neat woman.

"So what!" he said irritably, feigning indifference. "It's that overgrown Marcia James, that Luella Larson, and that Becky what's-her-name type. Nobody of any consequence or — "

"Pardon me," interrupted Newton. "Whitlock, are you calling Marcia James 'overgrown'?"

Alan realized at once that "overgrown" was not the right adjective to describe old Chuck's true woman, but before he could amend bad work, Joe whispered: "There he is! Right behind them!"

"Well, will you look at that!" Newton exclaimed in awe, apparently having already forgotten the slur to his love. "You were right, Joe. I didn't believe it; I knew Wigwam was daft, but — "

The sight was horrible but real. Cantering up beside the girls was Wigwam Tuttle. He was talking to them from below, so to speak, while they giggled back at him with their awful, girlish yak.

"What is it?" Alan said, still disbelieving. "A Saint Bernard dog, or — "

"It's a burro," Joe told him solemnly.

"That's what I thought."

Wigwam had spotted the three lonely footmen. "Yahoo!" he screamed from that distance, loud enough to

18

make horses shy and neighbors stick heads out of windows. He dug his heels into the burro's fat sides until the little animal broke into a gallop and the guy reached his buddies before the Pony Belles rode by.

Once there, Tuttle jumped off the burro's back, ran forward, and collapsed at the feet of his three friends. He was face up, with his tongue lolling out. "Made it!" he slobbered with these fake gasps. "The Pony Express has got through ag'in, Gov'nor. Water, for the love of heaven! Stench m'wounds, Corporal Whitlock, an' pull out a few of these arrows, please, sir?"

Alan saw the girls riding by, still laughing and waving. He tried to catch Becky's glance, but she had already turned away and was massaging that horse's skull between the ears. Then they were gone, the trotting hoofs kicking up dust on the road shoulder.

"Agh!" said Alan once more.

"You say something, Corporal?" Wigwam asked, sitting up while his untended mount strayed off to crop the lawn grass. "Y'reject the last words of a dyin' boy who has rode his best ride even when scalped by Injuns this-a-way?"

Alan met the guy's insane eyeballs for a second while reflecting that Tuttle was the only character around who could do the twenty-five foot rope climb upside down, or chin himself while hanging by his feet from the horizontal bar. People had almost forgotten his real name, which was Perry, but nobody knew why he was called Wigwam. He had a thatch of tight little brown curls all over his skull and even part way down his neck, and he'd built up arms and shoulders with bar bells and stuff until they were out of proportion with those of other humans. Nobody rejected dying messages from Wigwam Tuttle — at least nobody in Lamagra High School's sophomore class.

"I —"

"Forget that!" Wigwam said, springing to his feet with no hands. "Have you characters given any thought to the

19

approaching Lamagra County Fair? Have y'considered the Junior Gymkhana an' Rodeo?"

Nobody had, particularly since those festive days didn't take place until early August and there was plenty of stuff right here in June to think about. The Fair was interesting, though. Various Future Farmers of America and 4-H types exhibited their nutty projects in agriculture, such as hamsters, Belgian hares, Merino sheep, Poland China pigs, and so forth.

"Not exactly," Newton told him. "Why? Should we do it?"

Wigwam shrugged his wide shoulders. "Naturally not. Unless you plan to enter an exhibit. I've got my entry settled, is all. My blooded, trained burro, and —"

Alan had forgotten the burro. Now he froze with horror; the animal had strayed into his mother's prize double-ruffled petunias and was moving toward rosebushes, munching his way.

"Wigwam!" he snapped. "Get that burro out of our yard!"

"Here, Xenophon! Here, Xenophon!" Wigwam called. Then he whistled. "He won't come, Alan. He must like petunias. Usually he comes when I whistle that-a-way. But you can see for yourself —"

Alan didn't wait to hear the rest. He ran across the yard and seized Xenophon, first trying to lead and, that failing, to carry him away. He had his arms around the creature, trying to lift him, just as Aunt Ava and his mother came out on the porch.

His aunt's voice carried all the way to the flower beds. "You see, Alice," she cried, "he's exactly like his Uncle Val. Look at the dear boy out there. Why, he loves animals. That boy needs the companionship of a horse —"

Right now, in full companionship with a burro, Alan succeeded in hoisting the beast out of the petunias, where both of them stood panting from the heat of the battle.

"A horse, Ava?" Mrs. Whitlock was saying. "I don't think — "

"That's exactly what I said," Alan heard Aunt Ava declare. "A horse. That boy is a born horseman, and if you hadn't forgotten everything we know about boys, Alice, you'd have seen it yourself long ago. A car? Ridiculous — "

Mrs. Whitlock looked toward her son. "You don't intend to take that burro into your room, do you, dear?"

"No, Mother," Alan said. "I was just — "

With that, the two women went back inside; they had done women's work, probably.

2:

ONE BAD symptom of this deterioration that Alan had noticed was in sleep; he couldn't seem to do it any more the way he'd been able to when he was just a little freshman kid. It was practically dawn — around nine thirty — and he was wide awake but still too exhausted to move. Somewhere in the house feet stamped around walking, sitting down, that big stuff. It was probably Dorothea or that dog. Neither had consideration. Did they stop to think how a brother had been awake all night and only gotten eight or nine hours' rest? No! Not them; they weren't that kind.

He tested a muscle here and there; then a spine. Not bad; he could still move. For a while it worried him and then he suddenly remembered why he felt this crazy exhilaration. Aunt Ava had finally returned to Tulsa yesterday, by turbojet from San Francisco. Lately a lot of these silver sky ships had been exploding in mid-air, with no survivors.

Alan hoped nothing like exploding had happened to his good old aunt. An energetic person like her deserved to go on living into her second hundred years at least. Also, Uncle Hugo would be worried if she didn't come back, although owning a big mess of oil wells and stuff probably kept him fairly worried anyway, so Aunt Ava's absence wouldn't make too much difference.

Nine or ten times during her visit, Alan's aunt had described her delicate romance with Uncle Hugo. It was one of those May and December loves which began when he'd swept into the hospital to get another hunk of his stomach hacked out. Aunt Ava was superintendent of nurses and in the give-and-take of getting restored to ruddy good health, love had bloomed for Hugo Hulbert.

That was love for you, Alan thought; a person never knew where it would hit hardest.

According to Aunt Ava, the reason Uncle Hugo hadn't been in Lamagra on this visit was because he had to go to Washington to see a few Senators he knew fairly well. He wanted to get less confiscatory taxes on oil wells, so that the price of gasoline might eventually be lowered and help out the consumer. Uncle Hugo was a big man that way; he had a soft spot in him.

Recalling his aunt's departure had a psychological effect on a guy; Alan realized suddenly that he didn't feel bad at all this morning. He was up to merely awful again, and it seemed fine to have that kind of strength come surging back.

He crawled out of bed, showered, and dressed. Then he stood in the center of his room a minute to look around. An idea had struck him that he had the pure mechanical mind; his parents would have to admit the truth.

"Look, Dad," he could say, "maybe Aunt Ava was partly right; the ordinary youth shouldn't have a car too early because it does ruin grade standings."

He thought of a couple of examples in sophomores who had been ruined, like Joe Nunez for one; and Wigwam, who was pure wreckage, although he didn't have a car yet — only that silly burro. Also, it would be hard to prove that Tuttle had gone into rubble from any previous condition that was better.

He decided to forget examples, especially when he remembered that Leroy Walker made practically straight-A grades and whipped his Sprite over the road noon, night, and morning — generally in the company of similar slobs in the sports car set, a select circle around school.

23

No, he'd leave out personalities and simply demonstrate that car ownership improved guys who had been born with the mechanical mind. Right in this room he could show his dad that a son had the pure machine-brain. There were those powered racing car models he'd built when he was young, the propeller-driven planes hanging from the ceiling like dusty pterodactyls, a plywood working model he'd constructed to show the principle of the differential for driver education, and one or two personal inventions of his own. His favorite had been that solenoid door lock which would open only if you said the password into the mike. His mother had made him disconnect it, sure, because she claimed she couldn't yell the password loud enough to get in to clean. Besides, a person's mother yelling passwords didn't help secrecy and Dorothea could open the lock any time she wanted with her Brigitte Bardot throat whisper.

Then there was his automatic bookholder and page-turner for reading social studies in bed upside down. Who but a guy with the mechanical mind would have thought of that? Well, not many, his dad would have to admit.

Other kids had kept their brains on stuff like raising and training animals, such as their dogs. Wigwam had owned a batch of wild game pigs until a couple had broken loose and turned up rooting for acorns in the Veteran's Memorial Building. A few Legion members had insisted it was an insidious plot to undermine the post, until Wigwam went down and confessed guilt. They made him get out of the wild game pig business right then as punishment, but the guy claimed in private that it was a relief. There was a bleak future in game pigs, Wigwam declared; nobody would want to shoot at a pig with so many deer around. Guns could hurt a pig.

Alan was of a different stripe in sophomores. Right from the start he'd stayed away from animals and stuck with machines, mainly because he was a true Whitlock, he supposed. Mr. Whitlock had stayed away from animals too, except for a couple of dogs and stuff. He'd grown up on a ranch near Yreka, California, and was one of the few native Sons of the Golden West not related to Leo Carillo, Sutter, Frémont, or General Pio Pico. Or so he liked to say. He'd had his fill of nature back in youth. Now he claimed he got his full supply of it just by leaning over a red-hot barbecue pit a couple of times each summer and inhaling the crazy charcoal smoke.

His dad would come around eventually to some car sense, Alan felt sure. His mother would be another problem, but he'd find some angle — like offering to do all her errands and promising never to drive over fifteen miles an hour on the open road.

"Mother —" he could begin, "I realize I'm probably your son, and —"

His reverie was gradually undone by a pounding on his door and these bestial cries he finally recognized as Dorothea's. Alan stepped on the manual switch he'd installed to operate the solenoid and the door came open.

It was his sister all right, but she was different this morning. "Brother of mine," she said sweetly, "our mother would like you to come to breakfast as soon as you're ready."

For a second he stood there with jaw agape. Something was wrong with that girl. She smiled every now and then, sure. But not sweetly like this. Also, people seldom told him to do something when he was ready; usually it was the other way around — do it when they were ready.

"What's the matter?" he asked in alarm.

"Nothing's the matter, silly," Dorothea told him. "It's just that breakfast's ready, and — and Mother is waiting for you."

Alan hesitated, sniffing deeply. At least that part was true about breakfast. He could smell the waffles and maple sirup, the sausages and toast. A guy had to risk falling into their trap or starve to death in his own room. Besides, there was always the chance that a miracle had happened during the night and Dorothea had changed.

He put it to the test. " How's that thing you call a dog today? "

" Oh, King Aztec's fine," Dorothea chirped. " He's been asking for you all morning."

Alan's eyes widened. " Really? " he said incredulously, although he wouldn't have been surprised at anything that dog did. " Like, ' Where's Alan? ' In English, I mean? " It was impossible, of course, but having a talking dog around the place would add interest.

Dorothea giggled; she liked the idea too. " Of course not. He's just been sitting up and wagging his little tail every time your name was mentioned. That's all. A dog talks that way, and — "

" Who's been mentioning my name? " he asked suspiciously. " Dad? Or Mother? "

Now that he thought about it, the whole family had been acting strangely toward him for the last couple of days. They'd sort of stared at him as if he were going to get what he had coming sooner or later.

" Daddy's gone, and Mother — " Dorothea's tone changed. " I'm you're one and only sister, aren't I? " she asked.

He thought that over a while; something *was* up. " Sure," he told her slowly, " you're my sister I guess. But that doesn't mean I'm related to that stuffed mouse you call a — "

As he'd expected, that girl's phony reserve broke. " Don't you dare call my dog a stuffed mouse, Alan," she said, " or — "

A sardonic grin twisted his lips. Life, after all, was normal; here in this warm American home, surrounded by his loving family, he was still safe and secure in his position. At the bottom, that was, one notch below King Sinaloa Aztec II. That was where they thought the American youth

26

should be these days — just below sisters and dogs. He struck out toward breakfast with calm assurance.

His mother was in the kitchen pouring batter for a new crop.

"Good morning, Alan," she said pleasantly, "sit down; your waffles are almost ready."

"Thanks, Mom," he told her appreciatively and sank into his place at the table where they generally let him tie on the feed bag.

Every so often he used to take a quiet look at his parents to see how the erosion of time was getting them. Now he did the job on his mother for the month of June, and he was astounded by nature's quixotic trickery. How Aunt Ava and his mother could be real sisters he'd never know! Considering her age, Mrs. Whitlock was fairly neat and she looked as if she enjoyed being a guy's mother. She didn't have these piercing eyes like Aunt Ava's, which jabbed their knitting needles right into a person's skein. Old Uncle Hugo didn't have it so fine, and a wave of compassion for somebody bowed down with oil wells and Aunt Ava engulfed Alan.

Four waffles got done and his mother put them on his plate for a starter. Lately he'd had a picky appetite and he supposed she'd noticed a son's waning health. He doubted whether he'd need more than a couple of batches but he didn't want to worry her ahead of time.

Between waffles he began to glance around and he noticed Dorothea staring at him with a peculiar intensity. Beyond his sister, he could see the stuffed dog-mouse sitting up and pretending he had some gratitude and humility. When Dorothea wasn't looking, Alan bared his teeth in a soundless growl so fierce that The King had to blink and swallow hard. At least that was some satisfaction.

"Mother," Dorothea said abruptly, "are you or aren't you?"

" Sh! " replied Mrs. Whitlock. " Let him finish breakfast, dear."

" He is finished," Dorothea said. " Or at least he should be. My goodness, Mother, you said you were — "

Alan fixed that girl with a dark and wary eye. " What are you talking about? " he demanded.

Nobody answered. Mrs. Whitlock opened the iron and extracted more waffles, arranging them neatly on a plate, which she set on the table. Then she poured herself a cup of coffee and sat down, while King Aztec flipped his little head back and forth nervously, watching everybody and everything — figuring the percentages.

" Alan," his mother began, " I have — " She took a new start. It must be a difficult subject. " We have a surprise for you this morning. You see, the man called from Solvang and he's on his way now. You remember that afternoon when Aunt Ava and I drove down to the Santa Inez Valley? "

" Sure," he said. " I remember."

Who didn't? It was the only afternoon during his aunt's visit when anybody got a little peace and quiet. Even his dad had relaxed, remarking about how restful the day seemed.

" Well, we went to the Happy Meadows Ranch. That's a ranch down there — " smiling.

"Tell him, Mother," Dorothea interrupted. "Don't drag it out. Please! Please! "

With delicate deliberation, Mrs. Whitlock sipped more coffee. " Dear," she said finally, " there is a proper way to do everything. One doesn't blurt out, you know. One tries to act — well, civilized. A girl should especially, because — "

" What is this, mother? " Alan asked blankly. Yak, Yak! They did it, young and old.

There was an instant of breathless silence.

You might know it; Dorothea wasn't civilized. " It's a

horse," she blurted. " The man called from Solvang two hours ago."

Alan chuckled mildly and jabbed King Aztec's eyeballs the way Aunt Ava had jabbed his. As he understood the problem, somebody was lugging a horse around. He felt sorry for the poor guy because being saddled with a horse in this day and age was probably like going to Lamagra High School and being a sophomore.

" Sure, sure," he said absently, " a horse! " He turned to his sister. " Dorothea, don't blab out like that. Act civilized, why don't you? "

" It's true, Alan," said his mother in a sort of rush. " The man called and he's bringing the horse. That's what we've waited to tell you. It's a surprise and your sister is a little excited. We're all excited about it."

It didn't surprise Alan a bit, knowing Becky and those Pony Belles. Probably all over the broad United States of America, women were excited about horses, and guys had to lug the equines this way and that to get them to the old corral. He shrugged.

" What's so big about that? " he inquired.

" Alan! " Mrs. Whitlock exclaimed in a shocked tone. " Is that all you can say? Why — why, it's one of the nicest things Aunt Ava could do, and I don't think you should be so ungrateful. She wanted to help you and she went all the way down to the Santa Inez — "

A chill swept through Alan. Maybe this meant that his aunt hadn't made the plane after all and was down in Solvang less than a hundred miles away, riding home on horseback. It didn't sound too logical; somebody here was mixed up.

" I'll take him if Alan doesn't want him," Dorothea cried. "Mother! Please let me. Oh, please — "

Mrs. Whitlock sighed profoundly. " Children! This will do. Your father predicted that — Oh, never mind. If Alan doesn't want the horse, we'll simply have to return him and explain to Aunt Ava as best we can that — "

29

"Horse?" Alan said, blinking. "What horse?"

"Your horse," replied Mrs. Whitlock with dignity. "'My Buddy' is his name and the man is delivering him quite soon now. I've asked your father to come home as quickly as he can, but if — "

Alan was rising slowly from his chair. He'd heard of these nightmares which made bad dreams more real than genuine life, and — "Horse?" he said, his voice shaking a little. "You mean a real live *horse. Here?*"

It was actual life, all right.

"Yes. Aunt Ava realized that was what you wanted most when we saw you out there in the yard lavishing your boyish affection on that little burro, and — "

"Can I ride him?" Dorothea pleaded. "Let me ride him this morning, will you, Alan?"

He hadn't heard. Slowly he folded back into his chair, trying to grasp the big picture. "A horse!" he whispered.

"A real palomino," Dorothea shrieked. "Oh, isn't it wonderful, Alan? You'll never need a car now. You can — We can ride him to school together every day. Oh, Mother, can I get one too? I mean, I'll save and — and do all the dishes, and — "

"No, dear," said Mrs. Whitlock gently. "One horse will have to do for the present until we see how My Buddy gets along with us, and — "

"Well!" said Dorothea bitterly. "I might have known it. Alan gets all the horses; he gets all the fun! Everything. Yet is he grateful? Look at him, Mother! Is he glad the way I'd be if I had a horse? No."

For once his sister was right. Truthfully, Alan Whitlock had no emotion whatever as the news of Aunt Ava's largess gradually sank in. His first reaction was that it had to be a joke, but nobody was laughing. Mainly, he was stunned, so he merely sat there like a dynamited fish without thinking or even breathing. It was all he could do to wiggle his gills.

Yesterday he'd been a guy with the mechanical mind

who had nothing but the ordinary horrible problems. To-day his kindly aunt had sent him a live horse!

He tried to imagine what sort of animal a person would pick out to mail to a nephew, but every time he got the horse-vision it began to look like Aunt Ava herself, and no real equine could do that. Also, where would a guy in his condition keep a horse? No matter how he tried to brush the idea away, he kept seeing this enormous Percheron-type steed with him there in his bedroom fighting for equal space. It wouldn't work out.

" Aren't you going to say something? " his mother asked in that half-worried, half-accusatory style mothers have. " Don't you want a horse, Alan? Your — your father said — "

In the Whitlock family a person learned how to accept a gift, from a bedspread to an elephant. A guy took the thing with a smile and claimed he'd been wanting it all his life. So if he got a horse, he said he'd been dreaming horse, eating horse, wanting horse ever since he began to think — which obviously wouldn't be too long ago. After-ward when noboby was looking, he stuffed the gift into his dresser drawer, where it could keep getting in the way of things he really needed. A horse wouldn't be exactly like that, but he had to go through with the ritual.

" Sure — " he began. " I'm crazy — "

He meant about getting this neat present from Aunt Ava, but right there he stopped cold. A pickup truck had pulled in front of this house right now, and hitched on be-hind was a silvery blue two-horse trailer.

" Mamma! " Dorothea said in a whisper. " It's — "

Anyone could see what it was on the truck's cab door was the legend: HAPPY MEADOWS FARM and underneath was lettered: WELL-BRED HORSES FOR HAPPY OWNERS.

Mrs. Whitlock was already standing; now she undid her apron. " It's the man from Solvang! " she announced in her businesslike voice, the way women get when a package has come from the department store and they know they have to sign a receipt. " You see, Alan — "

31

He could, all right; seeing was easy. Believing was the part that was difficult. There was a tall, lean character getting out of the truck and Alan watched him with a transfixed fascination. The guy had on a tight shirt and jeans that looked as if they'd been tailored on the Western plains by true prairie dogs. He stood beside the open door a moment, fumbling in the seat for something, and then walked out into the middle of the street and pushed back his big hat to stare at the houses. Mr. Fegley, the next-door neighbor, came out on his lawn to help stare, probably. Finally, the man in jeans walked around in back of the trailer and looked inside.

Dorothea had been holding her breath. Now she gasped: "He's coming here. Oh, Mamma! He's really looking for us!"

"Of course!" Mrs. Whitlock announced blandly, as if people with two-horse trailers had been dropping in regularly all her life. "That's the truck and trailer from the Happy Meadows Farm."

It proved the whole Whitlock family could read. Alan sat deathly still while the lone cowboy booted his way across the lawn. He certainly had the tan of the open range and the hard, rawboned look of an *hombre* only a couple of weeks out of Tombstone, Arizona. "Howdy, ma'am!" he'd probably drawl. "Ah'm a'hankerin' t'sashay up to th' Whitlock *remuda* an' undo th' bowline on th' Western hackamore o' this here hoss-critter your Honeybelle Aunt Ava — "

He'd reached the porch and pressed the doorbell; the deeptone electronic chimes belled forth. King Aztec II began to yap furiously in his squeaky barking voice, protecting stuff.

"Alan — " began Mrs. Whitlock; then she hurried to the door herself. "Hello," she said.

"Mrs. Whitlock — yes?" the tall stranger asked with an accent, probably from Wyoming or someplace. "Outside I got a fine little horse. You were expecting a horse this

32

morning — yes? " The cowpuncher sounded more like a Dane; everyone around Solvang came from Denmark — even the cattle — so Danish cowboys figured, naturally.

Alan's mother nodded and signed something. A few minutes later they all went outside and watched while the old cowhand dropped the trailer ramp.

Well, a guy couldn't help noticing the long, white, silky tail and the delicate head turned around to stare with those huge, thin-lidded, far-apart eyes, and the little ears pricked forward intelligently.

But it wasn't until the whole animal stood there before him in the driveway that Alan realized this was a horse who was all horse. The midmorning sunshine caught his coat, burnished with the golden hair against a darker chestnut, and the light platinum mane and tail rippled in sheeny contrast. Gently, fastidiously, he moved to the edge of the driveway and cropped a few early asters from the flower garden and munched them thoughtfully. Then, still nibbling, he looked right at Alan and held him with his gaze.

Deep emotion stabbed through Alan Whitlock. Never in life had anything alive seen into his secret self quite the way that horse had done. Why — Those huge eyes were filled with sympathetic understanding and sorrow for the way the world did a horse and a guy. But a horse planned to keep going and help his master all he could; a horse had nothing else to live for.

Alan stood perfectly still.

" Where shall I establish him? " the cowhand inquired. " You have perhaps a corral. No? Then maybe a pasture? Not that? "

Mrs. Whitlock sounded nervous. " We don't have anything yet," she replied, " but my husband will — " She trailed off. Please tie him by that tree — the one near the garage. That e-elm tree. It's nice and cool there."

The Copenhagen cow-waddy shrugged; he seemed

33

somber, almost funereal now that parting was close. " You
have hay? " he asked. " Some grain, maybe, like oats? "

" We have a lot of oatmeal," Dorothea offered.

" Sh! " said her mother. " No. Nothing right at present.
My husband will take care of that, I'm sure." She smiled
brightly.

The Dane from Solvang shrugged once more. In silence,
he led the gorgeous creature past Alan and into the back
yard. Tethered to the elm tree, the horse began to tear into
the grass at once, but turned frequently to stare at the
people still standing in the driveway. His ears were pricked
forward and a questioning look appeared upon his noble
brow where he had a star. He had an even blaze running
down his elegant nose, where fine nostrils blew out as the
puzzle deepened. Evidently the grass was tasty; he moved
slowly about, cropping it and showing four near-perfect
half stockings.

Still without a word, the cowhand unloaded a light
Western stock saddle, a colorful blanket, and a single-
reined bridle with snaffle bit. These he set near the garage.
Then from the truck he produced a small pitchfork,
stepped inside the trailer, and emerged with an enormous
load of hay, which he carried back and tossed against the
side of the garage within the animal's reach. He put the
fork back and replaced the trailer ramp.

" He'll need water and plenty more feed," the man told
Alan.

Dorothea was awed by the wonder which had come into
her young life. " He's so *beautiful!* " she now whispered.
" We could call him Sunset Gold, couldn't we, Alan? "

For the first time, the Happy Meadows man spoke with
great positiveness. " You shouldn't," he said heavily. " Already his name is My Buddy. Already somebody else tried
to change his name to Cinnabar." The cowhand shook
his head with what might have been infinite pity. " Better
to leave the name he likes himself. Better to — " He seemed
on the verge of delivering himself of a profound mystery

34

about this horse, but he said no more. He stopped and sighed; then squinted away to the hills and the flawless sky as if he thought it might rain.

"What — what does he like to eat?" Alan ventured hesitantly. It was the first time he had spoken since the horse arrived.

"Eat? A horse?" said the man. "Why, grain, oat hay, little alfalfa. Anyway, the best. He likes that. Otherwise — " He didn't finish. "Well — "

"Thank you so much," Mrs. Whitlock told him. The interview with Danish cowhands was over.

The man nodded, got into the truck, and drove off. Halfway down the block he slowed and looked back. It seemed to Alan that he shook his head in what might have been doleful rue, but who could tell what a Danish cowboy was thinking?

"I'm going to call him Sunset Gold anyway," Dorothea said. "Sunset Gold! Sunset Gold!" she called in a caressing voice.

The horse had moved over and was eating the hay, about half of which was already gone. He didn't even look up; it proved he had a healthy appetite.

A strange power seized Alan Whitlock. He whistled softly and called, "My Buddy," in a quiet tone.

The animal dropped a whole mouthful of hay. His strong neck came up on good shoulders and he turned his sensitive Arabian head, with nostrils flared and ears pricked forward. Then it happened; he whinnied right at a guy — the same as horses did on television. It was as if he said: "I'm here, master of mine, awaiting your slightest command. Ride me! I'll work for you, stand by your side; I'll be your sworn companion through thin and thick."

Suddenly, Alan Whitlock's throat grew hard and spiny until it hurt. He began to walk forward in a kind of daze — toward his buddy.

35

3:

Mr. Whitlock reached home about two minutes after the family mother telephoned the news. He came screeching into the yard as if he'd really burned up the road.

Alan was still in the back yard with My Buddy, getting acquainted by feeding him handfuls of the hay he was missing, while Dorothea and King Aztec kept trying to mess in.

When his dad approached, Alan glanced up, but he was too excited to notice Mr. Whitlock's expression. Later on he was going to remember that on the first meeting his father looked serious, if not somber, to find his only son in the company of a genuine horse.

The man was dressed in his regular business uniform of course — slacks, and the wide-checked sports coat that had his Toastmaster's and Lions' Club buttons glinting from the lapel. He didn't appear to be too equestrian-minded at the moment.

"So the old — I mean, so your Aunt Ava really did buy you a horse!" he said, as if he were as surprised as anyone.

"Yes, Dad," Alan told him, grinning with pleasure. "And do you know — Why, I never thought I'd like to own a horse, but — "

Mr. Whitlock said something under his breath. But it couldn't have been what it sounded like. Immediately afterward he did a peculiar thing for somebody who was man-

36

ager of the Lamagra Guarantee Loan Association. He waded in close to My Buddy, patting him on the neck and moving his right hand across the shoulder and down the foreleg while the horse stood perfectly still, head raised and nostrils quivering. Slowly Alan's father lifted a foreleg while at the same time he shoved the horse slightly off balance with his left hand.

He dropped the hoof while My Buddy glanced around appreciatively and swished his long tail a couple of times. "At least he's been shod," said Mr. Whitlock, adding, " on that foot. We won't have to call the blacksmith for a while. Alan, a horse needs to be shod at least every six weeks. That's oftener than a boy needs shoes, you know."

Until now Dorothea had been keeping a discreet distance, but with her father here she came up close on My Buddy's off side, so that the animal turned and glared at her suspiciously. "Isn't he wonderful, Daddy?" she said. "Aren't we lucky? Isn't our horse the most gorgeous thing that —"

"Not *our* horse," Alan corrected sternly. "My horse."

"Isn't Alan's horse beautiful, Dad?" she said wistfully.

"Oh, my yes," Mr. Whitlock told his daughter warmly. "There's nothing quite like having a wonderful, gorgeous horse around the average American home. I tried to tell your aunt that we need this horse the way the U.S. Government needs —"

"Needs what, Daddy?"

"Nothing," replied Mr. Whitlock grimly. "I was simply thinking out loud, I suppose." He passed his hand in front of his face, sniffing deeply. "Not bad," he commented to the bright summer day. "A fine country odor. Nothing smells so much like horse as the real article." He turned to Alan. "Well, Alan, we'll have to get busy —"

"Busy?" Dorothea asked, crestfallen. "But aren't we going to get to ride him, Daddy?"

"I presume so," said Mr. Whitlock. He appeared to square back his shoulders resolutely. "But before you do,

37

there are certain small essentials connected with horse culture. You should know that, Dorothea. Aren't you a Girl Scout?"

"Sure, but Girl Scouts don't know any — "

"I don't suppose they do," her father said, a little sadly, Alan thought. "A horse has to have someplace to live. He needs — well, a lot of things young people don't take into consideration when they — they yearn to live on horse-back — "

Dorothea was genuinely alarmed. "Can't he live here with us?"

"You mean, in the house?" Mr. Whitlock laughed once, but it struck Alan that his father needed to get some sincerity into his merry mirth. In a way it sounded more like a sob. "Dorothea," he said in a kindly voice — only he was looking straight at his son, "a horse — even a light horse like this one — needs a stable or at least a stall. He should have some sort of corral, and pasture. Also — "

"Couldn't he sleep in the garage?"

The man seemed to shudder. "No," firmly, "he may not sleep in the garage, Dorothea. He wouldn't like it in there, and furthermore — " Mr. Whitlock stopped and sighed — as if the subject were almost too big to discuss.

His father's attitude surprised Alan because now that he thought about it, the garage was the logical place for My Buddy to bed down — at least for a while. "Then what'll we do with him?" he asked.

"We'll have to board him for a time, Alan," Mr. Whitlock said. "That's been my intention ever since I learned of this insane — or rather, this fine gift of your Aunt Ava's. We'll board him until we can — " he looked off toward the hills and maybe into the future when the Whitlock acre became Alan's Horse Ranch with My Buddy leading the herd with his piercing stallion scream — "make other arrangements," he finished. "I understood that a certain R. B. Gimpel up on Crispin Road boards horses."

38

"That's miles from here," Dorothea gasped, as if she had just learned that she had a cruel father.

"It can't be helped," he told her firmly. "We'll go telephone now." With that, he started for the house. Dorothea trotted along beside him while The King circled them both.

Alan remained behind to give one final bundle of hay to his horse. "Don't worry, boy," he whispered. "About an hour ago I thought I didn't need a horse either, but I do. I need you a lot."

Then he followed them toward the front door. It had been a long time since his dad had known a horse, he guessed, and it might take a while for My Buddy and a guy's father to get acquainted. It had begun to look sensible to board the palomino for a few days until he could build a nice stall and other stuff a horse would enjoy. It wasn't more than four or five miles up to Gimpel's; a youth could walk that far in the morning, pick up his faithful mount, and return at night when the work was done.

Mr. Whitlock was on the phone when Alan came in. "Operator," he was saying, "I'm told that the telephone at R. B. Gimpel's has been disconnected. Can you tell me why? I mean, is Mr. Gimpel still in business?"

A moment later he hung up. He sounded panicky. "She doesn't know. Those operators never know anything."

"Are you sure there's nobody else listed, Tom?" Mrs. Whitlock inquired with a wife's sweet reasonableness.

"No. Nobody in Lamagra except Gimpel has undertaken to board nags. And Gimpel's gone!" He swung around to Mrs. Whitlock. "Not that I blame him. You and your sister might have investigated horse-boarding facilities before you —"

"Why, Tom!" said Alan's mother, shocked. "You've known for days that My Buddy was coming —"

"I've known, but I don't think I really believed. Besides, I counted on Gimpel."

There was silence.

"Why don't you call Dr. Bison?" Dorothea's voice suggested girlishly. "He's a veterinarian, Daddy. He'd know everyone who boarded horses, because he boards dogs and cats and — and things — "

"You could call Dr. Bison," Mrs. Whitlock said thoughtfully. "Dorothea, that was a wonderful suggestion — "

Five minutes later Mr. Whitlock put down the phone again. "I knew this town was backward," he announced to nobody in particular, "but just how far back I hadn't realized. Here we are in the last California central coast county that has any open range, with horsewomen and sheriff's posses all over the place, but does anyone have the business acumen to board horses? No! Bison claims the nearest place is the Los Osos Stables in San Luis. That's twenty miles away — "

"That's exactly how far Sheridan had to ride," Dorothea said hopefully. "Miss Sickles read us a poem in social studies — you know, the one that keeps repeating 'with Sheridan twenty miles away.'"

"Please, dear!" said Mrs. Whitlock. "Your father is trying to think."

Alan glanced at his dad, wondering how she could tell; when a son was trying to think, nobody noticed. Mr. Whitlock did have a sort of concentrated expression, but it could easily be a bad toothache.

His father stood up. "Nobody boards horses," he observed in a hollow voice, "and I'm late with a couple of business appointments." He stared out of the window with a moody eye. "At least the weather's perfect," he said. "I'll run down to Grosshalter's Feed and Garden Supply and get some — a bale or two of oat hay. Alan, you'll have to stake that animal out in the back lot tonight. In the clearing." He spread his hands in a gesture of resignation. "Later on we'll think of something."

A son had to nod in appreciation; there was a father for a guy! Sooner or later Mr. Whitlock always thought of the way to handle emergencies. If horse boarding houses

40

were closed, he figured a better angle. His dad was the sort of man the old-time cast-iron youths grew up to be; they took care of stuff even if it killed them.

Sure enough, he left and was back in a few minutes with two bales of hay, which he unloaded out near the garage. " Get him off our lawn, Alan," he suggested mildly. " Stake him out with that long rope you'll find hanging up some-where in the tool shed. A good cool place would be under those oak trees. See that he has about half a bale of this hay and plenty of water. You can put the saddle and other gear in the garage, and — "

" Tom? "

It was Mrs. Whitlock. Father and son turned from horse plans to find out what she wanted.

" Yes? "

" A Mr. Howard Hagenfield just telephoned. Do you know him? "

" I do. Did old Hagenfield leave a message? "

Alan's mother spoke like the courier of good tidings. " He said he couldn't wait any longer, and besides, sitting there in your office he'd had time to think clearly, he said. He's going to invest in the Stufflebeam paper. Does that mean anything to you, Tom? Do people in Lamagra in-vest in paper? "

" They do occasionally," said her husband with all the gay good cheer of a professional pallbearer on his way to the job. " Hagenfield was going to buy the unsalable paper on that miserable old Masonic firetrap. I've only been working on him for a little old month. Now — The Stuffle-beam mortgage is handled by that skinflint, Linnell, at the American Bank, and — It's merely business; the breaks of the game. Hagenfield would use my office to think in. Any other place he'd have gone on in his usual style: Think-less Hagenfield! "

" I'm so sorry, dear," said Mrs. Whitlock compassion-ately. " I suppose it has been a little distracting this morn-ing." She plucked a couple of sprigs of oat hay, which

41

were still stuck in the hair of Alan's dad. She was always helping out.

"No bother at all," the man told her. "I like to be sure your sister's horse is comfortable."

He grabbed a broom from the garage and swept a lot of first-class hay from the back seat of the car. Then he got in, waved good-by, and took off.

Well, that was the business world, Alan realized. His dad couldn't get his mind off the romance of the work, probably.

He devoted the remainder of the morning to finding a good spot for My Buddy. There was a fairly level cleared space on the hill's approaches that had a low property-line marker driven deep into the hard shaly soil. To this, Alan attached an eyebolt where he could tie the rope. Thus his horse could wander around in a wide circle without becoming entangled, although Alan had to chop down a few bushes that would have been obstructions.

Afterward he staggered up with plenty of hay and strewed it around in convenient locations, although he knew his dad was certainly wrong about how much breakfast food a horse could eat. Opened up that style, a bale turned out to be an awful quantity of hay. A little horse like My Buddy probably couldn't get away with it in a whole week. Yet it made a son feel glad he had a generous father who didn't want a guy's steed to stand around starving to death in the midst of plenty.

Dorothea watched him work for a while, begging to ride. He explained to her patiently that a person took care of the needs and comfort of his horse before he'd do another thing. Books even said so.

As Alan recalled it, every story about horsemen made that brutally clear. A man could ride into the trading post after he'd been in the saddle day and night for a week and had maybe been shot through the spine and had a couple of busted legs to boot. Still, although it might be a hundred degrees below zero outside, he got his trusting horse into warm quarters, cooled him with exercise and a brisk rubdown with the salt bag, prevented him from drinking too much water, and then saw that he had the best rations possible. Only then would he consent to having a blood transfusion himself.

Mrs. Whitlock called Alan and Dorothea in to have lunch, but before they left, he patted My Buddy's sleek coat and told him what a good horse he'd been. Also, not to make so much noise when he gobbled down his hay.

Right there he learned why a person was supposed to talk with a horse even though it was a dumb animal. The palomino looked around and seemed almost ready to reply. Alan wouldn't have been too surprised if he'd said, " Thanks a heap, pardner," although naturally he didn't. Few equines talked English, although they were probably smarter than some teachers.

All through lunch Dorothea kept right on pleading for a chance to ride, so immediately afterward Alan lugged the saddle and bridle up the hill.

He'd never saddled a horse before in life, but he'd watched the job done a couple of times. To his delighted surprise, My Buddy stood perfectly still while he adjusted the blanket and then hoisted up the saddle, pulling in the cinch snugly.

But it was when he lifted the bridle that he had to decide he was a natural-born horseman and hadn't known it all this time. My Buddy took the bit as if he liked it better than hay and would have put on the bridle himself had Alan suggested the idea. He stood there ready to go, with his thin-lidded, beautiful eyes glancing around as if he was proud to be alive and happy that he lived here with Whitlocks.

Alan put his foot in the stirrup and discovered at once that the cinch needed to be a lot tighter. " Sorry," he explained. He'd been thinking of how a guy felt when he wore a necktie, but My Buddy wouldn't want his saddle slipping off.

At last he mounted and rode. He knew at once what they meant to be free on the open range — a guy born to the saddle. My Buddy could almost read his mind, turning with the slightest touch of the rein, stepping out smartly with grace and confidence. Merely by leaning forward a trifle and touching the horse with heels, they broke into a trot when they reached the field adjacent to the house.

Alan noticed that trotting wasn't so fine; with almost no urging, they broke into a smooth gallop for a short distance. Then he turn proudly and rode his horse up to the back door.

" Mother! Dorothea! " he hollered. " Come and take a look! "

But it was when his sister was riding that he learned My Buddy was really special. That horse was completely aware he was carrying a delicate girl with no inborn horse brains. He pranced along with exquisite care, slowly and gently, and when the ride had gone on long enough he came back.

" He won't gallop! " Dorothea complained. " And he won't go where I tell him to go."

Alan didn't reply, but down in his heart a fine, warm emotion was growing for his Aunt Ava. It proved how some people could get misjudged. Maybe his aunt was a born superintendent of nurses, but she certainly knew how to select a smart horse.

Later in the day, he rode in the direction of Wigwam's house. The Tuttle residence was over on San Jacinto, across Lamagra Creek and up the slope opposite Oak Hill. Going there Alan learned more horse facts because part of the time he had to ride on fairly well-traveled roads. My Buddy wasn't the least disturbed by cars; he acted as if the machine age wasn't even here yet, although he seemed to be looking both ways when they crossed Main Street. It almost was the other way around because that horse bothered automobiles. People gave them plenty of clearance as they passed in their hurly-burly rush to get to business.

From a half block away, Alan knew Tuttle was home because he could see the guy out in his yard burning trash. Wigwam's burro was there with him, helping out by eating trash too good to throw away.

Wigwam merely stood there amazed while Alan dismounted and tied his horse to a handy apple tree. Xenophon cocked long ears and let loose with his characteristic burro whoop, but My Buddy pretended not to notice anything unusual. He had poise; he stood there calmly and ate a couple of green apples for taste.

"Where'd you get that critter?" Wigwam demanded, finally.

Alan told him briefly. "Tell you what, pal," he finished, "saddle up your burro and let's go for a ride."

It turned out that Tuttle didn't have a saddle; burros, he claimed, were too sensitive for anything but bareback riding. The guy gave his trash a final poke with a rake and then walked all around My Buddy like a judge at the County Fair.

"Not bad," he grunted. "For a horse, that is. Naturally, Whitlock, you realize that a palomino can never be a burro no matter how hard he tries?"

Alan grinned. "Sure," he said. "Now come on, Wigwam. Let's ride. Put the cover on the trash burner and let's go."

It took quite a bit of persuading; Wigwam claimed that his burro was such a high-strung animal that he might take exception to traveling in the wrong company. At last, "We'll chance it, Whitlock!" he said. The guy was game, all right.

A few minutes later the two friends were riding together up one of the sandy roads near the summit of San Jacinto Hill. From there they could look down and see most of Lamagra spread out before them.

"This is really living," Alan said, glancing down from

where he sat, horse-high. Wigwam's burro was practically scampering along beside him. For some reason he recalled a story he'd read long ago about this Don Quixote and his pal, Sancho Panza, who'd gone out together to find some tilting windmills.

"You're right," Wigwam told him, "as far as you go, Whitlock. But owning this kind of transportation takes quite a bit of care, know that? Of course, there's less with a blooded burro —"

"Like what?"

"Well, like a lot of hay and grain. About a ton a month for that horse of yours. Now take a burro — he's more of a compact type. Like these economy cars."

Alan tried to think hay in ton lots. The idea was so big that it was ridiculous. That was Wigwam for you; the guy's mind was sprung in some vital part which made him exaggerate everything about an even dozen times. He didn't dispute the wild idea. "Yeah! Yeah!" he replied, chuckling. "A ton of hay a month, and —"

"Some horses eat more; some less," Wigwam continued airily. "Each horse has got to find his own average." He stopped. "Hey — take a look. Wild life."

Ahead of them a curving road crossed theirs. At the juncture, a jack rabbit had come scuttling out of the brush to dive for safety on the other side. Immediately afterward, both youths heard girlish laughter.

"Women," Tuttle hissed, "chasing poor little jack rabbits."

A moment later Alan's heart froze. Coming into the road were horses — three of them, ridden by girls whom he recognized instantly. Pony Belles! Becky Linnell was in the lead.

"Whoa, Xenophon!" Wigwam screamed. "Here come them cossacks!"

More girlish laughter. Women had a peculiar sense of humor.

"Why, Alan Whitlock," Becky sang out as soon as she

46

was near enough, "where did you get that absolutely yummy horse! " She was coming closer. "He's — he's perfectly marvelous! "

The next moment she had reined in beside him. Alan paid no attention to Tuttle, who was yelling at the other girls not to startle his high-spirited burro so they'd have a runaway on their hands. Not two feet away from him was the one and only true woman in this whole wide world. She was smiling while the light breeze tangled her short hair; her direct blue eyes stabbed right through him with their crazy little lights.

This was a time to say something suave, between horses, so to speak. He searched his brain for an easy, witty remark; nothing there. "I — I — " he began, making a good start at least.

My Buddy picked that time to turn in the road. He wanted a good look at Miss Moonfire. In the movement, Alan brushed against Becky. "Pardon me! " he croaked. " I didn't mean to — " His face was aflame, he knew. Sunburn had got him.

She didn't seem to mind; instead, Becky leaned over and patted My Buddy's neck. "He's wonderful! " she said. " Will you let me ride him someday, Alan? "

He thought that over a while as the other girls drew near.

"Sure, Becky," he told her deep in his throat. "Any time; any time at all."

And you knew it, man; a guy didn't really exist until he owned a helpful horse!

4:

It was just before dawn one week after the arrival of My Buddy. Had there been a living human creature awake to observe the Whitlock kitchen, he would have seen a dim figure move stealthily in the stark half-light.

There was a living creature in there observing, but it wasn't human: it was King Sinaloa Aztec II up early as usual to watch dogs and people. With his tiny head cocked first to this side and then to that, he perceived Mr. Tom Whitlock creeping around in the act of preparing a businessman's breakfast. Like all Aztecs before him, The King was genuinely fond of Mr. Whitlock; the man was all heart.

Despite the abnormal hour, the head of the household was fully dressed, ready, evidently, for the take and give of the Lamagra Guarantee Loan trade, since a loaded brief case stood beside the door. To King Aztec II, it doubtless smelled like an unfriendly but departed pig.

Right now, Mr. Whitlock was in the act of pouring into a bowl those sucrose-saturated chips of the ruddy natural corn which, as everyone knew, was America's favorite breakfast.

Even so, the man was obviously lonely and distraught as The King pattered near on delicate feet. It might have been that dog's intention to lick the paw of a fine old master as if to say: There, there, old hound! I understand.

48

Things are rough all over for us dogs — especially for displaced Chihuahuas.

It wasn't to be. King Aztec II couldn't reach anything to lick because of a frustrating size differential and was, besides, in peril of being trampled. So, still unnoticed, he retired once more under a small wrought-iron planter, where he was relatively safe. Something was up around this place in addition to the faithful family canine.

Mr. Whitlock poured milk, which instantly unsaturated the sucrose but caused no sparks to fly from sugary magic. He sat down and began to sop up the tiger nourishment a man demanded for one more day of free enterprise.

Only The King saw a new shadowy figure enter: Mrs. Whitlock. Not being a woman to go sneaking around in the dark for any purpose, Mrs. Whitlock snapped on the light.

"Tom!" she exclaimed, yawning her surprise. "What in the world are you doing up at this hour? Why, it's only a little past five!"

"Daylight-saving time," said Mr. Whitlock, blinking. In the clear light he saw what he had been eating and pushed it away. "I'm simply having an early breakfast, dear," he said with stiff dignity. "I didn't want to awaken you because you were sleeping so soundly. I thought you might be — well, tired from your — your jolly afternoon of riding yesterday on that infernal horse."

"Well, my goodness!" said his wife somewhat petulantly. "I *was* tired, dear. Almost everyone is at five in the morning. Then *you* came out here and began clattering around." She poured herself a cup of coffee and sat down opposite her husband, tasting the brew speculatively. "It's awfully strong, isn't it? Did you — did you wash the coffeepot?"

"I made it on a base of last night's coffee."

"It doesn't seem that recent," Mrs. Whitlock mused. "I don't know what happens to coffee. It — does it combine with the metal or something, Tom?"

"I thought it entirely acceptable," replied Mr. Whitlock, squelching scientific inquiry. "I liked it; there's body to that coffee."

She tried another sip and nodded in complete agreement. "Body, certainly," she said with that little gay note of wives who can go along with the mood, "but whose?"

Her husband didn't reply; instead, he looked pained. Abruptly, Mrs. Whitlock reached across the table and patted his timeworn hand; worn, that was, from assigning time payments on first mortgages. "What's the trouble, Tom?" she asked in a sympathetic voice. "This isn't — it isn't like you to be up at five, brewing your own coffee, munching prepared breakfast food. Why, you once told me you thought the whole trouble with American education was the sending of children to study math with nothing but corn chips on their little stomachs!"

Mr. Whitlock stared out of the window and into the breaking day. "Well —" he said at last, "if you must know, it's that horse. For the entire past week I've been devoting most of my time to the welfare of a vain, unpredictable equine, and —"

His wife's lips formed that tender little smile of women who are married to wonderful, wonderful men who know not their own towering strength and endurance — and do not wish to know. "Of course, dear," she said compassionately. "You helped Alan build the corral and box stall. My —" her eyes grew veiled, "how proud I was of you both when you took our boy — our little boy, Alan — down to see about ordering grain, oat hay, wheat bran, and — and all those things. You're — you're fine, and good, Tom, and —"

"— and the Lamagra Guarantee Loan Association is about to go down the grain drain. At least it's tottering with that assistant I have — Wellington P. Smith — at the helm. Smith's a financial jitterbug! He thinks the U.S. dollar has been pegged to the Mexican peso as a good-will gesture, I believe —"

50

"But our son Alan — "

" — and Alan is *not* a little boy, my dear. Let's not live in the past; he's nearly six feet tall and quite capable of — "

"I know, Tom! He's so much like you!"

Mr. Whitlock's eyes widened in what might have been horror. "I believe you think so!" he declared. "Well, I have to get down to my office at once and do about a week's work in twenty minutes or so, else — " He made a slicing motion across his stomach, roughly in the region where an honorable but disgraced samurai plunges the hara-kiri sword.

"Now, now, Tom! It can't be that bad."

"You're so right! Of course it can't," replied Mr. Whitlock. "But it is! And why? Because of that irascible horse and your sister, Ava. By ' irascible,' I mean prone to colic!"

His wife looked shocked and surprised, the way the English do when circumstances are rather un-British. "Why, Tom!" she remonstrated. "I believe you don't like My Buddy. I think you're — I think you're jealous of a horse. A — a dumb animal."

The charge was nasty but true. "I am," he admitted grimly. "We might as well draw the lines here and now. I am definitely anti-horse, and particularly anti that one. Alice, you may set me down here and now as favoring the machine as a better way. Why — why, I trust our rotary power lawn mower more than I do that dumb creature, and I'm certain it will contribute more to the common weal — "

"Well, my goodness, why shouldn't it? All My Buddy has are — " Mrs. Whitlock paused. "The common what?"

"Weal."

"Oh, I thought you said ' wheel.' You were talking about machines and they have wheels, naturally. And if you expected that poor little horse to have — Well, you understand what I meant, don't you?"

"Perfectly," agreed Mr. Whitlock, who knew in advance when he was licked — which was always. "But don't call that nag a 'poor little horse,' Alice, and mark my words, no good is likely to accrue from ownership of that beast, handsome and well-fed though he is." He snorted. "I've never seen a vainer horse. He knows he's handsome. He revels in it!"

"You *are* jealous!" Mrs. Whitlock replied, clucking her tongue. "And, Tom, you're tired from getting up so early in the morning. Why don't you go back to bed for an hour or two until your disposition —"

"My disposition has nothing to do with it," Mr. Whitlock announced haughtily. "I simply won't have a horse — even an intelligent horse — running my affairs. Is there something unreasonable about that? For thousands of years, my dear woman, mankind has been struggling upward through the mire of — of the Augean stables to — well, toward progress and products. Now you, Dorothea, and that — that foolhardy boy have elevated a — a *hippus* to a managerial position in our — our destinies!"

He paused, reconsidering his words; there was rhetoric in them, all right, but also a trifle of effulgence. My Buddy was not actually in the house yet, pushing buttons.

"There's been a little confusion, dear," Mrs. Whitlock admitted slowly, "but now that's over. From here on, Alan will do everything. Actually, he'd love to. Only yesterday he told me he wished you'd stop hogging all the time with his horse, and —"

Mr. Whitlock's eyes glittered dangerously. "He said that, ha?"

"No — no — no-o! Not exactly," she amended hastily. "He said he *wanted* you to have plenty of time with My Buddy, I should have told you. He thinks that as a boy you were probably horse-starved, as he put it in his colorful teen-age jargon. He believes you didn't get enough affection from your — your family horse, or —"

The man shut his eyes and groaned. Nothing more.

"Besides, Ava and I took all this into consideration, Tom," she continued hopefully. "We realized there would

52

be a few days of adjustment, but after that — Well, you read the survey yourself. In high school after high school, educators are finding that owning a car is going hand in hand with low grades and — and even delinquency."

"Educators!" sighed Mr. Whitlock faintly. "I suppose now they want a horse in every classroom. Yes, I suppose it figures; only a short time ago it was to be educational television."

"Tom, why can't you take me seriously?"

"Oh, but I am," said Mr. Whitlock. "So tell me this. Do educators, as you call them, have any statistics on the effects of a horse on the boy? Especially of a horse like that prima donna out in the old corral? Do they?"

"Tom Whitlock!" she exclaimed. "How can you talk like that about an innocent and wonderful animal you know nothing about? Both Ava and I were born in Texas; we rode horses almost as soon as we could walk, and we know —"

Her husband's eyes narrowed. "In my time I've been acquainted with a couple of nags myself," he said evasively.

"Work horses. You said so yourself. An old white mare and four or five —"

"Horses, nevertheless. There's much to be learned from a work horse —"

"Well, if you know so much, what's wrong with My Buddy?"

Mr. Whitlock looked trapped and confused. "I said he was a prima donna."

"Why shouldn't he be?" his wife rejoined. "He's beautiful, and he's spirited — the sort of horse who will bring out the noblest qualities in our son."

"Noblest qualities?" The man had to blink. "Why? Why should a horse bring out anything in a human being — except sore muscles?"

She laughed gently with a trace of pity and a smidgen

53

of scorn. "Ha! Ha!" Mrs. Whitlock giggled. "And you say you know all about horses!"

The guiding hand of the Lamagra Guarantee Loan wavered. Mr. Whitlock stood up uncertainly, and after brushing off an errant corn chip or two from the brim, put on his hat. "I didn't say I knew *all* about them. I simply — well, sense that there's something not quite sound about that critter. He's — flighty — or perhaps 'opinionated' would be a better word. He's a showman of some sort, like a — like a fancy diver or a male ballet dancer, or —"

"Piffle-paffle!"

"What was that?"

"Piffle-paffle," replied his sensible wife, "or, as we used to say when we were young, Tom, horse-feathers! You're just imagining these qualities in My Buddy because you're — Well, a man who has been doing desk work as long as you have forgets what he may have known about horses." She saw him head for the front door. "Why are you leaving so soon, dear?"

With his hand on the doorknob, Mr. Whitlock turned back to her. "I want to get away long enough to earn a few dollars before that horse gets up," he said. "If I don't leave, he'll want something from me."

For emphasis, he put his foot down and by chance the shoe toe landed beneath the wrought-iron planter. "I have a certain obligation to the investors in —"

"Yap! Yap!" King Sinaloa Aztec II announced to the invader.

Mr. Whitlock jumped nervously and peered down into the void. He saw the household dog. "You shut up!" he snarled by reflex action. "Go back where you came from!"

Instantly The King recognized the creepy blood scream of the great bull ape and took off for safer hide-outs. Let some other faithful dog stand guard. Meanwhile his ungrateful master glared after him, sensing triumph over at least one segment of the animal kingdom, small though it was.

54

His passion was short-lived. His wife was already beside him, pecking out a pitying kiss. " My! My! " she cooed. " Hims is really snappish this morning, isn't hims? First hims doesn't like perfect horses; next hims hates itty bitty puppy dogs."

" Oh, stop that, Alice," said the breadwinner. He backed away out on the shadowed porch toward a couple of crusts. " I'll be home late — much later than usual. Don't wait dinner."

Before she could reply, he had skulked off, aware, as must be all weak men, that the victory was as hollow as a butterhorn. A breadwinner needed a hot dinner after a day of juggling miles of money. As he drove away a winsome whinny put music into the morning.

That welcoming sound aroused Alan, and though not truly awake, he bounded out of bed glad to be alive so early. As he dressed he was still aware of two pleasant dreams from which he had been awakened. In the first one, he'd been young again, say around twelve, and had sent in one of those soap-wrapper puzzle solutions and had actually won the Shetland pony.

The second dream had been about Becky Linnell. Alan had seen the frightened girl on a runaway horse. By reckless and daring pursuit on My Buddy, he had snatched her from harm's way just before she plunged over the precipice. " Thanks a lot," Becky had told him in the dream. She loved him.

Of course there weren't any precipices in Lamagra County and dreams were misleading. Besides, real life wasn't so bad. He went to the window and pushed aside the curtain. Sure enough, out in the corral a trusty horse waited. The morning sunshine displayed My Buddy in warm silver and live gold.

" Hi! " Alan said quietly. Last week he would have denied that anyone could feel this way about a horse. Now —

A few minutes later he reached the stall and spent some time rubbing My Buddy's nose along the blaze and talking

55

with him. Because the horse kept nuzzling him and motioning toward the feedbox, he dished out a nourishing breakfast for a pal.

It was about one fourth of the suggested daily ration for a thousand-pound horse at medium work, and consisted of three pounds of oat hay, two pounds of grass hay, a pound or so of rolled barley, three fourths of a pound of oats, and a half pound of wheat bran.

As Alan watched My Buddy gobbling down the feed he reflected that his dad hadn't been too enthusiastic about hunting up barley, bran, and oats. Mr. Whitlock had insisted that many a horse had lived the rich life on oat hay alone.

It had been only after quite a bit of discussion that the man had come around to the Light Horse Project manual style of thinking. He'd said: " Oh, all right. All right, Alan," the way he did when he grew tired of fruitless argument. " Give him his daily bran, if you insist."

When a guy's horse had a healthy appetite like this one did, maybe it proved that the younger generation knew something about feed at least. Once or twice right now, My Buddy glanced around happily and swished his tail a couple of times, so that it flicked Alan.

He laughed. " Stop that, old pal," he said fondly. " Take it easy."

My Buddy pawed the ground a couple of times in reply; it was amazing how a smart horse could answer a person without wasting words.

Finally Alan decided to amble into the house and find out how breakfast for humans was getting along. He headed that way, whistling happily. This would be the first day he'd have his own horse all to himself.

For the whole past week his dad had kept messing in, messing in — building the corral fence, putting up the box stall, and rushing between home and office. A guy's father had to be that way, Alan supposed. They had a lot of residual horse-fever left over from the time they were boys

56

themselves and the automobile was young. They probably wanted to get in and relive their youth. Well, he hadn't said anything; a kid needed to use tolerance and wait patiently while his dad grew up.

At the kitchen door he turned for a last look before going inside. The stall opened into the corral and he could see My Buddy there in the shadows, lapping up the last of the ration. The pride of ownership swelled through him again with an emotion a guy wouldn't dare discuss with anyone else; he had to feel it for himself alone. And to get that emotion felt back at him by a perfect horse — well, it was an experience no youth could afford to miss. Alan didn't blame Mr. Whitlock for having a little horse-hunger left over from those days in wild Yreka; nobody wanted an underprivileged dad.

He squared his shoulders and went into the house. There were a couple of details about My Buddy that he planned to work out today. By now he'd grasped the absurdly wonderful knowledge that some guys were just natural-born horsemen. He was one of them, give or take a point for the fact that he owned a perfect horse.

Yesterday, though, he'd goofed and done something wrong. Today, Alan meant to think it through so he and My Buddy wouldn't get off on the wrong hoof.

He'd been riding on San Jacinto Hill again where, to his surprise he'd come to those crossroads at which he'd met Becky the other day. So he'd glanced up the road to the right, and sure enough, there she was riding with her girl chums of the Pony Belles.

As Alan sat tall in the saddle watching them, for some reason — maybe by mental telepathy between horses — Becky had turned and seen him. She'd waved and he'd responded with his heart thumping like one of these trip hammers, as they said. He'd had the sudden impulse right there to ride after them and speak a witty word or two in passing — maybe something like, " Great day for a ride, huh, Becky? " Of course that wasn't too brilliant.

Keen judgment had taken over at once. They'd already had one pleasant meeting yesterday. If he chased Becky now, it might appear to her that he was trying to press advantages by being a fellow horse lover. Well, he knew girls better than that. They didn't like a guy to be too brash. They could get bored with any little thing whenever it got too frequent and thus stopped amusing their sparrow-type brains. He'd made the merry chitchat with Becky already. Now let it go; let them come seeking the opportunity to yak.

"We'd best be riding home, pal," he'd told his horse, touching the rein; that was all it took with My Buddy.

At that moment some horse up the hill had taken the notion to whinny — probably Luella's nutty blood bay. My Buddy's ears had slid back when he heard the sound. Instead of turning as Alan had suggested, he'd wheeled full around and started up the trail after the other horses.

Right now, Alan had to chuckle about that. It was his fault of course; he'd given too much rein to a sensitive mouth. "No, pal," he'd said. "I did wrong. This way — " giving some rein in the right direction.

Well, he must have forgotten everything he'd learned in a week of horsemanship, because My Buddy had kept right on being confused. The next thing Alan had known, they'd ridden alongside the girls. He'd known he had to say something; he didn't want them to realize he'd befuddled his mount.

"Morning, Becky," he'd sung out, grinning. "Thought I'd run up this way myself."

"I'm glad you did, Alan, and — " Becky had replied, leaning over to pet the palomino.

Conversation had stopped right there because My Buddy had gotten the wrong message again and trotted ahead beside Luella.

It had been a little embarrassing, especially when Alan had decided to try again a minute later. That time, My

58

Buddy responded fine, turning and heading back. As they'd passed Becky, she'd said, " Oh, Alan, I've been meaning to — "

He hadn't found out what she'd been meaning to do because the palomino kept right on traveling even though Alan had reined in. Sometimes, he supposed, a guy's horse knew best. He'd swung around in the saddle. "Be seeing you," he'd told Becky gruffly.

At that the meeting had been fairly romantic. Now all he needed to learn was how to give My Buddy right signals next time.

" Oh, Alan, I've been meaning to — " he said softly within his own mind. In a way, he would like to have heard the rest; as it was, the statement covered a fairly wide range.

Next time would be different. There were only a few things to work out. Details.

5:

He LEARNED immediately that he was going to put off having an understanding with My Buddy until another day. This time it was Dorothea who messed in.

"Alan," she said as soon as he sat down for breakfast, and loud enough so the family mother got the message, "remember your promise!"

"What promise?" he asked with real intellectual curiosity because it was a general principle of his never to promise a sister anything of his own free will.

"Yesterday afternoon you promised I could ride My Buddy this morning. All morning."

Alan was genuinely shocked because Dorothea's words were untruthful, strictly forbidden in Whitlock tradition for generation upon generation. He was about to deny, but he suddenly recalled that he was his sister's older brother and that she was a fairly good kid, at that.

All last week she'd hung around the work, eager to lend a helping hand. She'd proved only too willing to snatch up a hammer and to nail fence boards. What did it matter that almost every nail she drove had to be yanked out and laboriously straightened? Also, when he'd said get some water, bring the salt, measure out some hay, Dorothea had been in there pitching all the time.

So he surprised himself; he tried to think of what could be the true basis of her delusion about promises — which was also pretty unusual for him. He guessed that horse

60

ownership got some maturity into a guy and cemented family relationships with a few half hitches.

Now he rememberd that he really had said something about letting her ride My Buddy all morning, only he'd meant some morning in about a month or after school got started again and Dorothea happened to be home with the measles or Sudbunny's Plague.

"Sure, sure," he'd told her in a kindly style after she'd nagged about two hours, "I'll let you ride him all morning someday."

Well, nobody liked this constant sibling trouble in the home and that was what Dorothea was — a little sibling. It was a kind of hard name to call a guy's kid sister, especially one as pretty and smart as she, but in a sense it fitted.

"I said you could ride him all morning — " he began in a mature horseman's voice.

"On Thursday!" Dorothea cried triumphantly. "And this is Thursday, isn't it, Mother?"

Mrs. Whitlock brought over some more food. "Yes, it is," she admitted. "Tomorrow is Friday."

Horse-handling taught a person to approach animals slowly and with these confident, kind movements so nothing got startled and kicked. It was probably the same way with people, especially women and girls. Within his mind, Alan made a fair comparison of "someday" and "Thursday." They didn't sound too much alike.

"I — " he began, choosing thoughts carefully.

They didn't give him the chance to be mature. "It's thoughtful of you to share, Alan," his mother interrupted. "Besides, this would be an excellent morning for you to hunt your job."

"Job!" he croaked, pushing out the dread word as much to get rid of it as anything. "What job?"

"Whichever one you want to take," Mrs. Whitlock said in a merry tone. "But I was talking with Mrs. Goulart yesterday afternoon at the grocery store and she said that

Mr. Goulart — you know, the one who owns Condorgas Service Station — had mentioned he might need a strong, willing boy to — " pausing, " to work, I suppose."

Alan gulped hard. Up around school, notably among sophomores, the Condorgas mentor was referred to as No-Pockets Goulart in car ownership chitchat. Chuck Newton had named him that, mainly because any credit or extra little consideration like a couple of pounds of wind from the free-air supply had to come directly from the man's bloodstream. He never gave away anything out-of-wallet. Working for him would probably undermine national minimum wage laws.

He held back a bleat of inward anguish just from hearing the Goulart name spoken by a relative. Besides, experience had taught him to hear out his mother's crazy schemes. Usually they had some firm foundation; he'd learned mother-placating psychology by listening to his fine old dad handle family matters.

Alan tried to yawn to show complete disinterest in job opportunities, but it came out like this dying yip of the beat generation. " Ha, ha! " he chuckled in glee. " What gave you the idea I was in the market for a job, Mother? " That should send her into research for proof, all right.

Not Mrs. Whitlock; she didn't even begin the hunt. From her apron pocket she dragged out a bunch of scrap paper. " These gave me the idea," she told him seriously.

He had to blink a couple of times to get the focus, but the papers turned out to be bills for various details of getting My Buddy fitted into the family scene. " But Dad said — " he began.

" I don't want you to bother your father about this," his mother continued. " He's awfully busy with — " she smiled, " with business. But these represent a total of over two hundred dollars, although we don't expect you to pay for the stall and fencing — at least not right away. And we're willing to advance you the initial feed costs, but from here on, Alan, you'll have to earn the money for My

Buddy's keep — or — or found, as we used to call it when we were girls — " She smiled again, somewhat archly. "The feed you now have will last about two weeks, your father says, and one week of that is already — "

"Down the hatch!" Alan blurted, recalling how a friendly horse stuffed in the stuff.

"Down the throat latch, you mean," Dorothea amended helpfully.

"It's not necessary to say it so crudely, Dorothea," Mrs. Whitlock said gently, in there training people all the time. "But horses have to eat, Alan. A horse owner must think of that first, and it wouldn't be fair to you if your father and I went on paying the feed bills. You wouldn't appreciate My Buddy nearly so much if we did."

That showed what they knew about appreciation, Alan thought in stark unbelief. A person would appreciate his horse a whole lot better if he didn't have to weigh out each grain of grain on the gold standard. It could lead to scrimping back a healthy ration and bring on colic or sleeping sickness in both horse and owner. He'd already heard My Buddy sneeze once and it was a scary sound.

He tried postponement from force of habit, the same way he did with trash so that when the hour came to burn waste material, a guy had enough to get his teeth in it and feed the flames.

"Hadn't thought of it just that way, Mom," he told her gamely, "but now that you mention it, the idea makes a lot of sense. A lot. I will need some cash to buy feed." As he recalled the outrageous price offhand, just straight hay was bringing over forty dollars a ton, and grain was the pure treasure of the Sierra Purina.

"I'll help out with some of my allowance," Dorothea volunteered.

It was mighty decent of her, Alan had to concede, although he realized she was merely making one of those dramatic gestures girls liked to fling around in your face.

63

Dorothea's whole allowance would buy My Buddy an after-noon alfalfa break about twice a week.

" No, Dorothea," he said. " Mother is right. I'll have to — to get a job and pay for the feed myself. But I don't think this morning is the best time to look. Next Monday would be better."

Naturally it turned out he was wrong; this morning was the ideal moment to seek a gainful job and there was no time like the present. At last Alan Whitlock understood that old saying about not looking a gift horse in the mouth; if a guy did, he'd see where all his hay-gold was going to disappear.

After breakfast we went out with Dorothea to the corral and saddled the palomino. Then, leaning against the fence, he watched his sister trot down the road with My Buddy dancing along with his silvery mane and tail streaming in the breeze and haloed by sunlight. For about fifty yards, King Aztec had scampered after them, yapping like a bantam banshee and anxious to get with hill and dale too. It was a long time since Alan had viewed such a horrible sight, especially when he had to chase that idiotic dog and drag him home on his mother's orders.

Later he set off afoot toward town with the intention of chuffing his shoes along the dusty byways of commerce. He hadn't counted on brute labor for any purpose this summer, although he was willing enough to work for the good of a happy horse.

However, in the back of his mind was considerable doubt of the job reality. Last summer, and this one too, a lot of the guys had gone around hunting careers without success. The demand for youths in marts of trade had proved slow; only a couple of people had found work and they were older, like seniors. Newton and Wigwam had talked seriously about employment in agriculture, like down at the Poultryman's Packing Plant, for example, but real poultrymen had already cornered the market. These days a youth had to grow up, get some brains and know-

64

how, and probably be married and have six kids of his own before they'd trust him to pack their precious frozen chicken gizzards for shipment. An untrained youth might drop a giblet every so often and ruin it.

The chances were strong that he couldn't get any job, not even with Goulart, because his mother had said that No-Pockets wanted a strong, willing boy. On the two or three occasions Mr. Goulart had invited Alan to get off his lot and fill his bike tires at some other station operated by a maniac, the Condorgas chief had not used that type of high praise for a customer.

Still, somebody was certainly going to have to pay for My Buddy's feed in summer and winter. That pointed up one of the main differences between cars and horses. If you weren't dragging town in a rod — thus sopping up the fuel — a car didn't stand around outside whinnying for petrol night and day.

In the next two hours of diligent job search, Alan scrupulously avoided Goulart's station on the outside chance that No-Pockets had actually gone mad on Condorgas fumes and was ready to hire a sophomore. He hit Safebuy Stores, three competing filling stations, two garages, and one drugstore. Nobody was hiring. The only bona fide lead he got was at Pennypacker's Ford Sales and Service. Mr. Pennypacker showed interest after he'd asked Alan why he wanted a job as a mechanic.

" To feed a horse," Alan had told him.

Mr. Pennypacker was leaning against one of his unsold new cars which had been designed by somebody who really could think big. " Now there's a new idea," he'd said, a little wistfully Alan thought. " I suppose there's a real future in feeding horses. Most people — "

But he'd let it go at that. " I'll call you if anything turns up," he'd finished. " I like to see a young fellow who's willing to work." It was a peculiar saying to come from a man with a son named Roger who was the fullback mainstay of the Lamagra football team.

Mr. Hawkins, who owned the Lamagra Bowl, was out of town. Some guy who said he was the assistant manager told Alan they might need a couple of pin boys later in the season, but they wanted them a little older. Twenty-one was more like the right age for pin-setting, the guy claimed. According to him, their finest pin boy was a married man forty-five years old who did the work merely for relaxation.

That about wrapped up the job scene — except there was always an opening on the delivery-boy staff of the *Lamagra Weekly Insider*. The trouble with that job, Alan knew by experience, was that delivering the *Insider* like mad every afternoon once a week netted a guy about a buck and a half monthly. Even so, Wigwam had bought himself the English bicycle he'd traded for part of his burro by pyramiding the proceeds clear from grammar school days. Wigwam said that all a guy needed to prosper at work like that was to save his pennies and let England muddle through by itself for about ten years.

When it was past noon he borrowed the telephone at Hayward's Drugstore and called home to tell his mother that work was at a standstill in Lemagra, no matter how high the crazy boom was shoving the merchandise to customers elsewhere.

He should have foreseen his mistake. "Have you been to Goulart's yet?" she asked.

When he told her he hadn't, she said: "Well, my goodness, Alan! Go down there right away. Why haven't you done so already?"

It was one of those trade secrets a guy couldn't explain too easily to a mother. She wouldn't understand that any employee of No-Pockets Goulart would probably be spoiled for other work in life and also lose so much face among sophomores that he'd be all haircut.

"I'll go there next," he said.

Trudging down that way toward the south end of town, he drew some comfort from the fact that with commerce

66

as flat as it was in the north end, the job at Goulart's was probably already snapped up by a gas engineer with a family.

The Condorgas symbol was a giant plastic California Condor about life-size, with its forty-foot wingspread always turned toward the breeze. It was mounted on a pole where its beady eyeballs could probably look out over the offshore oil lands down near Morro Bay. The rest of Mr. Goulart's plant wasn't so fine. It had gotten in the way of quite a few grease jobs.

From a block off he could see No-Pockets at work; the man had the build that went with a meaty neck and staring, hard little eyes. Alan shuddered; in a way, it might improve public relations to put Mr. Goulart up on the sign and let the condor pump the gas.

No-Pockets was dumping a tankful into a lady's car. The way the guy glared inside when he cleaned the windshield made a person feel sorry for her; she was earning her historic American right to refuel.

"You need a quart of oil," No-Pockets said.

The lady hesitated. "My husband doesn't want — "

"You still need a quart of oil no matter what your husband says," Mr. Goulart told her. "The most crucial instant in the life of your car is when I tell you it needs oil, see?"

The lady bought a quart. Meanwhile, Alan lounged around trying to look as much like another gas pump as possible and thus not attract unfavorable attention. He hoped neither Newton nor Wigwam happened to spot him in here treating with the enemy for even the ten seconds No-Pockets was likely to ask him to stick around and get comfortable.

The lady drove off, jerking in low, and Mr. Goulart watched her, shaking his head angrily. "They never learn!" he snarled to himself. Then he turned around and saw Alan.

"Who are you?"

Alan gulped and his jaw probably fell agape — a bad habit. "I —" he began.

"Then you're the Whitlock kid!" snapped No-Pockets. "Where've you been?"

It seemed a funny thing to ask a stranger. For example, did Mr. Goulart mean where had he been in the last couple of hours, or in the three years since Alan had jerked away his free-air business.

"I don't know," he said, meaning that he'd have to find out the question first.

"That figures!" said the Condorgas chief. "Well —" staring up into the flawless California sky where the plastic emblem wheeled, "I let myself in for this. Come on, you."

The main ingredient of the job turned out to be a substance called gunk. It took Alan about an hour of shoving the mops and stuff around the grease rack to realize he'd been hired.

"Three hours a day," Mr. Goulart finally slashed out, "and all day Saturday if I happen to need you."

The hours were chopped out of the center of the day when the Lamagra temperature was about a hundred and ten in the shade.

When the grease rack was done he got to gunk the driveway under the canopy and then Mr. Goulart started him out gunking the walls of the rest rooms. Mainly Alan had gunked himself; except for a couple of places on his shirt, gunk spoor was plentiful. At that, he hadn't minded missing lunch as much as usual; gunk sort of took the edge from a guy's appetite.

Quitting time finally arrived, although Alan figured he'd have to check a calendar at home to be sure this was the same week.

Before he left, Mr. Goulart told him the princely wage. "But you may be worth it after I break you in for a couple of months."

That's what he was going to be — broken in, Alan knew.

68

But right now the problem was to get home alive. He started out walking sort of sideways and up and down, using the last couple of muscles left that hadn't been permanently damaged by gunk. The style looked bad maybe, but it was survival tactics. He knew what those Congressmen meant when they said any increase in the minimum wage would cause unemployment. Probably for a nickel more an hour, Mr. Goulart would have made him commit suicide by gunking that much harder.

With unseeing eyes, he rounded a corner and passed a convertible parked there, and even the name THE GREEN GATE painted on the door didn't register.

A hoarse voice reached him. "Whitlock! Look alive — if you can."

Alan peered toward the car and made out familiar shapes. One was Wigwam and the other, Newton. He dragged himself in that direction.

"We saw you in there!" Tuttle said accusingly. "What are you doing around No-Pockets? Trying to catch leprosy?"

"Working for him," Alan gasped.

Both guys sat silent, apparently stunned by a pal's perfidy. "Then I was right, Wigwam," Newton said. "We've been watching you quite a while, Alan. I figured you were working, but Wigwam had another idea —"

"Forget what I said," Wigwam snorted. "A spy has to be smart. All I want to know is your purpose, Whitlock? Us sophs signed the oath in root beer to boycott that place for life, and here you are gunking for Goulart. You're a traitor, that's what."

Alan put his hand on the door handle, thinking that his chums might let him sit down before he collapsed from exhaustion.

"No! No!" Newton screamed. "Wait, you mad fool!" He sprang out of the car with some hunks of newspaper in his hands. Then he opened the door and spread out the stuff thickly. "Now get in and don't touch a thing. You want to ruin my upholstery by getting that gunk on it?"

Alan sat inside upon the newspapers, leaning forward to keep all parts of his person from contact with the actual automobile. Slowly, he tried to explain.

"Guys," he finished haltingly, "I didn't want to do it; you know that. But my mother says I have to earn the feed for my horse. It's the only job in town, and why No-Pockets gave it to me I'll never know."

"Because nobody else would work for him," Wigwam insisted.

Newton was silent. "A person can see Alan's side, Tuttle," he finally said. "Somebody has to buy feed for that horse of his and if his parents claim he has to work for it — he has to —" He turned around, putting his arm across the seat. "Keep away from the headliner too," he warned. Then: "I'll even throw some of my business your way. A gallon a day. I'll drive in and order a full gallon every day you're on duty."

"Thanks," Alan told him. He visualized a procession of sophomores coming into Condorgas and ordering one gallon. It meant he'd be with the firm about that long; one day.

Chuck started up the car and took Alan home, watching him all the time in the rear-vision mirror to be sure he didn't touch anything.

When they pulled into the Whitlock driveway, the tall guy got out and saw to it that Alan dismounted without rubbing against the doorframes and stuff, for which he couldn't be blamed. After that the three of them sat on the grass a while talking, and he noticed that where gunk was on his pants the grass died. Just like that. A little gunk touched ground and a whole patch of grass gave up.

"I've got the solution for you," Newton finally said, getting up and climbing back under the wheel of his car. "Why don't you enter My Buddy in the Junior Gymkhana and Rodeo at the Fair? Maybe you'll get lucky and win

70

a lot of prize money. You could feed your horse with that."

"Yeah," Wigwam added. "I told you I'm going to enter Xenophon in the burro-judging. He'll win the blue ribbon for the best burro in Lamagra County — you'll find out."

Nobody denied it, but they did admit that Alan's horse had to eat between now and August, when the Fair was held. A little later the two friends left.

At the back door Alan discovered just how fickle women are. His own mother, who'd made him get the job, wouldn't let him come in the house. "Go on out and feed My Buddy first," she insisted. "Then you can change your clothes and wash up in the garage. I'll put a clean T shirt, jeans, and things out there."

Painfully he made his way to the corral and saw his faithful horse come strolling up to the fence. "Hi," he said.

My Buddy approached, put his neck over the fence, and sniffed; naturally he smelled gunk. He drew back, nostrils quivering and thin-lidded eyes drawing closed.

That was the way, Alan guessed; in every life a little gunk. He went around to the feedbox and measured out the fifty per cent of the day's ration. Then he sat down on an old orange crate and watched his horse eat. He could scarcely move from gunk-back, but his brain still worked. As far as he could calculate in this diseased condition, the feed My Buddy ate right before his eyes now almost equaled exactly the day's wages.

That was ration 4 in the manual. Watching the grain and stuff disappear, Alan figured ways and means with a kind of desperation. Maybe if he tried ration 3, he could cut down, but as he remembered, that one figured out to twenty-one pounds too, the same as ration 4.

The palomino drank some water; then he slapped his tongue across the salt lick attached to the wall. That done, he turned with a horse's gratitude and whinnied at his master.

71

Alan sighed. That couple of swipes at the salt lick had cost him about five minutes in the gunk pits. So just when this summer had begun to look as if life would be worth being here, what happened? He'd gone and gotten himself a horse to support.

6:

A week later Alan Whitlock had aged alarmingly; one symptom was the way dawn got him. Nowadays he woke up every morning sort of by hearing the sun come sneaking over the horizon behind the Temblor range.

Today was no exception; the dim light brought him to full wakefulness. That made him question again whether thin horse eyelids were really a sign of intelligence, because in humans like himself it seemed to indicate a guy was stupid.

For a short time he fought off brutal alertness by pulling the covers over his head and trying to catch a little more sleep. It was of no use; he couldn't even rest, because he knew what would happen as soon as the full rays of daylight stabbed over the hills and down into the corral.

So he jerked the covers off his face and lay staring upward at the dark ceiling with burning eyes of fatigue. In about five more minutes, My Buddy would wake up. That horse had a routine he'd worked out that began with a soft nickering — the kind they talked about in books where the Western hero was out on the trail and his trusty horse kept telling him stuff. What those script writers didn't mention was the message the horse probably had: that it was around four thirty in the morning and time to hit the road. In a couple of seconds, the guy would leap out of his poncho and make the fragrant essence of boiling coffee mingle with the smell of the crazy purple sage.

It didn't work that way here. Around the Whitlock trail camp there was no messing with fragrant coffee first thing in the morning. A guy either threw on clothes and rushed out to pitch the hay or My Buddy went into the next step. The nicker became a full-fledged whinny, a sound on exactly the right key to penetrate the whole neighborhood. Night before last, Mr. Fegley next door had telephoned again. Instead of listening to Mrs. Whitlock the way he'd done the last couple of times, he'd insisted on speaking to Alan.

"Sonny," Mr. Fegley had stated, "have you ever heard of the humane society?"

Alan said he had, meanwhile picturing old man Fegley. The guy had big bushy eyebrows that could beetle down on a kid something fierce. Plenty of times in the past, Alan had come home the long way around just because old man Fegley was outside planting primroses, maybe. After a bad day at school with teachers, facing up to Fegley could tip a youth's delicate balance.

It turned out that Mr. Fegley was thinking about the humane society that protected people from animals. He was an early riser himself, the man claimed, but he liked to decide personally whether he was getting up or merely going to bed late. "Sonny," their neighbor had commanded, "you get out and feed that poor little horse. Nobody likes to hear a starving thousand-pound brute whimpering in the night. You keep him quiet. Otherwise —" He'd left it there.

In a way Alan couldn't blame him because after whinnying a while My Buddy might let go with the fierce, high-pitched scream of the wild inland stallion rounding up the herd.

The first time that had happened even his dad had gotten excited and gone charging around the house and into people's rooms to see if beams had let go and the roof was crushing the agony out of them. That morning Mr. Fegley had called up to inquire politely whether he should

74

summon an ambulance or do some other neighborly deed.

Well, as the manual said, every horse had its own distinctive traits and the owner had to know them and make proper allowances. Through kindness and firm treatment he could capitalize on the unique personality of his horse.

Alan groaned and stretched outraged gunk and gas-pump muscles. Yesterday Mr. Goulart had enjoyed a real run on lube jobs, and in the haste and waste of business had been fairly generous in throwing around the gupp-grease. Mopping black blobs behind an active employer could really keep a guy on the prowl.

He figured he had a whole minute more just to relax here while he thought things through, but he was wrong. From the corral he heard the nicker, which was really a sort of low neigh as if My Buddy were standing in the stall and chuckling to himself about all the good times he'd had as a young colt.

Alan groaned again, so pitifully he could have felt sorry for himself if he'd taken time to listen. Instead he sprang into action, dressing himself in darkness with the speed of a Marine boot with his drill sergeant hiding under the bed.

A moment later he was outside in the misty dawn where nature was on the tramp again. As usual the young quail stepped aside when they saw him stumbling up the hill-side; strong gophers dropped prize begonia tubers and dived for handy holes. The only woodland creatures who stood their ground were the sparrows out in the grain heaps who had long since figured the score: it was peace and prosperity for sparrows in Lamagra at last. This guy coming toward them was a bird's best friend, Alan Whit-lock, the barley spiller.

As he worked under the critical, thin-lidded eye of his intelligent horse, Alan's mind redesigned the electronic horse-hayer he was going to build as soon as he had a couple minutes of spare time. It would be push-button horse care. A solenoid would open the feed hamper and drop the exact amount of hay, grain, and bran into My

75

Buddy's feedbox. Then the door would close electromagnetically when the scientific amount had been fed. He'd already talked over the project with his dad, but Mr. Whitlock didn't seem too interested. What really held everything up was that Alan had counted on the man's giving an allowance advance to buy wire and so forth.

"It does a lad good to get up in the morning to hand-feed his pet horse," his father had said. "He — ah — he and the animal establish the rapport of personal relationship so — so necessary to — "

"To what, Dad? " Alan had asked.

"To expert horsemanship and good-neighbor relations," Mr. Whitlock had replied mysteriously.

Alan's father had heard a rumor that Mr. Fegley was getting up a petition to the City Council to ban the keeping of any animal larger than a Siamese cat — which would work hardship on plenty of Lamagra goats and stuff. "Don't allow that animal to screech that way again, Alan," he'd warned, " or we'll get sued for — And clean the stall and corral every day. Maybe twice a day. Otherwise we'll have the health department out here too."

"I do clean," Alan told him.

"You do not," his father had announced firmly. "I see more than you think I do. You've made a — a deal with your sister to clean the stall. She gets to ride My Buddy hour for hour, and — "

That was a person's family for a guy; no co-operation. It had been fair to Dorothea; she even said so. But no, his dad insisted he do the job himself. Not only that, from the time of their conversation, Mr. Whitlock personally inspected stable fitness every day. A clean stall helped make for a hygienic horse, the man insisted. "And a hygienic horse," he'd finished, " is a — a happy horse."

Done with feed chores, Alan now leaned against the stall and watched a happy horse gnaw down the grub, dollar by dollar, job piled upon job.

"Take it easy," he suggested softly. "Don't gulp so fast! "

My Buddy looked around with a sort of grin. He liked a master to take interest.

Alan considered speaking sharply about eating more than the manual said was good for a light horse doing light work. But the same thing happened to him that did every morning. He went soft; he couldn't be harsh to a horse.

Instead, he saw once more that he was the owner of an animal of good conformation. My Buddy's head was lean and delicately formed. His ears were small, alert, set close together, and his neck was strong, with good length. Also, his eyes were large and set far apart, and his shoulder was sloping with smooth power in the muscles, whereas there was plenty of depth through the heart.

His horse needed fresh water, so Alan went into the stall for the bucket that was held against the wall with snap locks. He moved in the correct manner, letting the palomino realize what he was doing by telling the animal so in a soft voice. " I'm here behind you," he said. " I'm coming in to get your silly water pail."

My Buddy looked around and nodded again, then returned to the grain. It was about time he got some fresh water.

Alan kept in close beside him, watching rear feet. The horse shifted a little just to keep in practice, maybe, but he didn't kick. So far he hadn't kicked at anybody, although the book said a horseman should always keep alert no matter what.

He got the bucket, stumbled down to the spigot, filled it, and staggered back with the cold water slopping down his pants leg and into shoes, naturally. When the bucket was back in place, My Buddy took a sloop from the salt block, a couple of snuffs of water, and went on eating. Those were his feedbox manners.

Alan allowed his eyes to travel along the animal's short back and well-developed hind quarters, noting for the hundredth time the strength of waist and loin, legs straight and of good bone, with strong, clean hocks. Furthermore, My Buddy's pasterns were long enough to be springy and flexible. In short, he was a close-coupled horse with plenty of heart and well let down; he was friendly and tractable, so that he could be ridden by anyone with a good seat and good hands. As Xenophon, the famous Greek horseman who happened to have the same name as Wigwam's burro, had once said, this horse was " kind, used to the hand, and fond of man."

The daylight had grown strong by now as My Buddy cleaned up the last of his grain and nuzzled around for more.

" That's absolutely all," Alan said, trying to make his voice sound confident. But when he realized his horse was down to bare wood and sampling pine splinters, he tossed in a few more handfuls. That went too. This horse had good teeth with the black spots and straighter angles that indicated his youth. It confirmed a guy's real suspicions: My Buddy was sort of a sophomore in horses — young, strong, and unwilling. Assign him a seat and he'd probably study algebra along with the rest of future science-cats.

Alan sighed profoundly. Listening to his horse chomp grain reminded him he hadn't had his own breakfast. Nevertheless he moved into the stall for daily foot inspection, although you'd think a smart horse could be expected to look at his own feet; but no, somebody else had to do it for him.

He proceeded in the prescribed style, working in close to My Buddy's near fore shoulder, stroking the silky coat a while and babbling softly about stuff a sensitive horse liked to know.

" You're the greatest horse in the world," Alan said. " You and I are pals. Now I'm going to look at this hoof of yours, pal."

He stroked his right hand down the foreleg while he kept his left at the shoulder. When he held the lower leg just above the fetlock, he pushed with his left. My Buddy leaned off balance and lifted the crazy hoof.

"Shoe's tight," Alan said, thinking toward the day when he'd need the price of a blacksmith, "and your hoof is clean." My Buddy looked around and pointed his ears that direction. He already knew about that hoof, apparently.

Next came the near hind leg, with the process repeated on the left or off side. With his hoof hook, Alan cleaned in the commissures from heel to toe around the triangular growth in the center called "the frog," probably by frogmen. There were no rocks there or injuries; none of this thrush mush. Just some dried mud.

That done, he got out of the stall after unsnapping the horse's halter. My Buddy backed smartly into the corral, ready to begin the day's work. There was a phase of life Alan shared with his horse; they both worked. But he sometimes wished they could exchange jobs. He'd rather carry a hundred people around on his back all day than gunk another grease rack down at Condorgas.

After he'd showered and dressed, he still had time to sit around and think for a good half hour before the rest of the family got up. Though days had grown hotter, at this hour the house was still cool, so he went outside to the patio and sat in full sunlight to keep warm.

He found the same breathless, empty quality to the still air that he'd learned to expect at this time of morning when nothing stirred, not even a mother mixing waffle batter. Behind him and inside the house at the plate-glass doors was King Aztec, wanting to get outside and participate. Alan paid him no heed; after all, he had enough animal to care for without worrying about that dog who walked like a mouse.

Up on the hill, My Buddy beat his way around and around the corral as if practicing the 1320 at school during track season. Every so often he'd stop and stare down at Alan to see if a horse's best friend was watching. Meanwhile, The King scratched frantically at the glass and

79

whined at a pitch just inside the human wave length of audible sound.

At last Alan got up and opened the door so the dog could get out. He hated to see impatient dumb beasts, although the thought struck him that if he had to get up so early to keep peace with neighbors, Dorothea ought to get up to maintain peace in the home.

The King found something that looked like the thighbone of a slain hummingbird and began gnawing it out in the middle of the yard. Alan resumed his seat and pictured the demands of the day ahead. First was his three hours with Goulart the Ghoul, his own private name for No-Pockets. Pure misery! The worst part was knowing that he slid back all the time financially, despite labors which made cleaning the Augean box stalls look like horseplay. Close arithmetic had revealed that My Buddy's daily rations exactly balanced wages, plus job depreciation of school pants and shoes added to an occasional malted milk to keep up human strength.

It made diminishing horse returns all the worse because by now Alan realized that the day My Buddy had decided to follow Becky and her Pony Belle sidekicks was not due entirely to incorrect reining. Incorrect training had something to do with it; of Alan, that was.

Captain Kournakoff, whom the book claimed was one of the world's greatest riding instructors, said that a person needed to " be with his horse " all the time.

No lie! By now Alan knew that unless a horse owner was with his steed, the guy was in real trouble. A couple of times he'd even asked Dorothea the casual question when she came in from riding. "Were you with My Buddy? I mean, the whole time? "

" Of course," that girl had answered. " And I'm still with him. I'm here, aren't I, and so is he. Otherwise we'd both be walking."

What he'd meant was did My Buddy turn when he was

80

told, back up, and do the little necessary details of being ridden by a human. But Dorothea wouldn't know.

By now the problem had even reached the bridle and saddle stage. Yet Alan had followed instructions to the letter, being kind, firm, and gentle.

He guessed that instructions hadn't been written for a horse like My Buddy with an owner like Alan Whitlock. More and more he'd begun to suspect that his horse was a lot like himself mentally — somebody who sat around thinking his own thoughts. The resemblance stopped there. Physically, and in having a nice personality, the palomino was perfect, but when a sophomore horse was ridden by a genuine sophomore, somebody won out in the brain game.

The winner was My Buddy. Now he was getting bridled only after he'd decided the bridling time had come. That palomino could turn away just when the bit was getting slipped between his young teeth, take a waltz step sideways, and stand there looking at a guy reproachfully with big sad eyeballs. Maybe he'd bat his thin lids a couple of times to show who had the true intelligence and who really could pick a proper time to ride around.

Getting him saddled wasn't difficult, nor was it easy, either. The Western stock saddle weighed plenty, to begin with. Hoisting it to My Buddy's back took effort even when that horse stood absolutely still — which wasn't often any more.

Since day before yesterday, Alan wouldn't have been too surprised if he'd ended up with the bit between his own teeth and that horse cinching the saddle girth around him. Oh, it was probably an exaggeration, but not so much, at that.

Then yesterday in an open field with nothing in the way for a hundred yards in all directions, that horse had shied to the left, blowing out his nostrils in a horrified snort as he did. Alan simply couldn't figure out why. Dorothea had

81

ridden him nearly every day too, and she hadn't mentioned anything unusual.

"Alan! Come to breakfast." It was his mother.

He had to snap out of it; a guy might brood forever about his horse while waffles got cold on the table. But he couldn't tell his family he had a problem with My Buddy — not after kicking up all the fuss about being mechanically minded and wanting nothing more than a car in life. They'd think he'd invented the idea merely to cast aspersions on an equine he didn't want — and that was the farthest thing from truth. He wanted My Buddy ten times more than the best car in Detroit. They'd begun making a couple of good ones there again lately.

Either way, though, he was licked, and the funny part was that maybe this was the real problem. My Buddy knew he held the whip hand — or rather, whip hoof — somewhere down in that horse sense he had. He probably intended to keep it that way too.

Breakfast was nutritious and took a person's so-called mind off the trouble for at least a couple of minutes, although Alan's mother robbed peace by telling him that Mr. Goulart had called and needed him at the station a half hour earlier. It meant that his free time this morning was cut down to worthless. No use to attempt an understanding with that peripatetic palomino now.

Neither Dorothea nor his mother wanted to ride this morning. It would be a good time to straighten out gear in the tack box his dad had helped build. Maybe he could rub a little saddle soap around to keep leather supple and fend off field mice; brighten up bright work, as the manual suggested. All that. He wandered out into the yard.

He was just in time to hear a nasty, ingratiating foreign car snarl ripping down this street, Cabrillo Terrace. Sure enough, an instant later he saw the flash of red and there was an Austin Healey Sprite with that creep, Leroy Walker, at the low-slung wheel.

Walker alone in that car was enough to chill a normal

82

guy's pint of blood, but today two girls were with him. They went by the house slowly enough for him to recognize both. Marcia James was on the outside, and between them, snuggled up to Walker, was Becky Linnell, her hawk-wing hair flying in the slipstream.

"Agh! " exhaled Alan, closing his eyes quickly until they could get gone.

It wasn't to be; he heard that Sprite's snarl grow slow and mellow in the pipes, followed by the howl of a turn in lower gears. They were going to do a second take of him, for laughs, probably. He shut eyes tighter.

"Hey, Whitlock! " sang out this musical baritone voice — music to be sick, sick, sick by. "Wake up! It's today."

Reluctantly, he opened his eyes. There in his driveway not ten yards distant he saw the Sprite had come to a stop. More, Walker and the two girls were dismounting. Alan could feel his face burn because Becky was in the lead and headed right toward him. She was so pretty she hurt; in a way, she was almost as gorgeous as My Buddy. It struck Alan a hard blow right then that he had about the same trouble with the woman he loved as he did with his horse: no meeting of minds.

"We happened to be driving by," Becky said, glancing around, "with Leroy, and we saw you out here, Alan. Can we look at My Buddy? "

Alan stared back at the corral. The palomino was out in full view. He supposed anyone here could look at him who wanted to, but — "I — "

"Oh, thank you. Thanks a lot, Alan," Becky said. The next minute both she and Marcia had scampered up to the fence and were petting that horse.

Alan stayed behind to find out what type of battle Walker was seeking. The guy thought he was good, rugged, and sharp; the only real trouble with him was how true that happened to be.

"Hi," Leroy mouthed, faking up his creamy smile full of these teeth while folding his fancy sunglasses into a

83

morocco leather case. " Heard you'd gone in for bit and saddle, stirrup, and hackamore, Whitlock. Not a bad horse you have there. Nice."

Alan turned that over in his mind, hunting the hidden trap. " Thanks," he ventured. " I like him myself."

" Mind if I look him over, too? " Walker asked with this false pleasantry. " Been thinking of buying myself a saddle horse. Used to own a couple when I was a little bit of a kid, but — Well, I guess I sort of outgrew horses, you know."

The guy was already sauntering up to the fence. When he got there he leaned close to Becky, scrubbing his silken paw all over My Buddy's face.

Well, if that equine persisted in a quixotic, playful turn of brain, now was the time to reach out and snatch off some vulnerable spot from Walker, like an arm or something. But did he; no! The palomino acted as if he adored Leroy immediately.

Alan reached the fence himself. Then Becky dropped this bombshelter, as they said. " Let me ride him, Alan," she begged in that style where if a guy refused, he might just as well go out and kill himself to save the state expenses. " Please? "

Before he knew why, Alan had agreed. Then his heart sank in the tank. It really wasn't up to him at all; Becky should have asked My Buddy the question, because only he knew the real answer.

Now, right here in front of everybody, including the one genuine woman in this drear world, not to mention Marcia and the town crier, Leroy, they were going to find out that he wasn't the master of this or any horse. It would be just like My Buddy to refuse the bridle on free-equine principles and run around in a circle just for kicks.

" Go ahead, Whitlock," Walker grinned. " Saddle him. I'd like to see a horseman at work."

The gauntlet had been flung, as stories put it. Alan scaled the fence and found the bridle. " Take it, for the

84

love of hay," he begged with silent eyes alone, advancing toward his horse with that firm determination the manual advocated.

Later on, he finally understood fully that he owned an unusual horse, one who was going to take quite a bit of study. My Buddy came up to him almost like a faithful dog and practically grabbed the bridle out of his hand. A moment later it was the same with the saddle; he seemed eager to get in there and pull his part of the load.

First Becky rode him; then Marcia. Finally, at Becky's insistence, Leroy mounted and took off for a turn around the half acre.

It was while he was gone and Marcia was looking over the stall layout that Becky really hit him with a surprise. "Alan," she said in a strange, small voice, " did you know that Stony Johnson is playing the lead in *Give a Man a Horse* at the Granada tomorrow night? "

" No," he replied, meaning he knew, but he didn't care much. He could take Stony Johnson and leave him; the problem was, where?

" You should see it," said Becky.

" I should? "

" Yes. Every horse owner should." She seemed nervous.

" Have you — I mean — have you seen it? " Being a horse owner, she should probably go.

" No, but I was hoping to."

He waited.

Becky seemed embarrassed, which usually didn't happen to girls; they had all this crazy feminine poise. " I was hoping somebody would ask me to go — "

She probably meant Walker. Well, no use to encourage her in dealing with that lump of chump. Let him ask for himself, the big creep. Who wanted to be that guy's Captain Pocahontas?

" Some boys don't ask a girl to go to the movies with them because they aren't driving a car — yet — " Becky said. " They — they don't realize that lots of girls are will-

85

ing to walk, especially with the — I mean, especially to a movie like *Give a Man a Horse.*"

It was an interesting side of life he'd never considered. "Is that a fact?" he asked.

She blushed. "Yes it is, Alan Whitlock!"

By that time Marcia was back and Leroy had come into view.

"Thanks," he told her sincerely, and went to unsaddle his horse, cool him off, and show her his fine horsemanship.

When he looked around, though, Becky was already headed back toward the Sprite. She was sort of stamping her feet, as if she'd gotten mad at him for handling My Buddy wrong.

That was women for a person; they were delicate and shy. But when they saw bad treatment to a horse, they could really flame, man!

7:

THE DAY turned up blistering and his stint at Condorgas had wrung Alan down to bare human rags of tags. Dorothea and his mother were in the house keeping cool. Even My Buddy drooped listlessly in the shade of the oak trees near the corral fence.

It was by now too late and too hot to undertake lessons in horse mastery, so Alan sat alone in the yard under a weeping willow tree. He was trying to think; naturally it was a case of no progress.

Mainly he couldn't understand why Becky had asked him to suggest to Leroy Walker about him taking her to the good movie. Sure, he loved her in silence and for aye, but there were some sacrifices even a love like his couldn't make.

So far he'd spent about an hour trying to solve the girl puzzle, with no results. Now he sat still, trying not to move so that he woke up more ants and sparrows. Thinking would get him nowhere; besides, Wigwam had called up to tell him he was riding Xenophon over. Around that guy and his sturdy mount, nobody did any thinking.

The afternoon droned on; King Aztec came outside without his sweater and stood around shivering in the heat. After a while, Chuck Newton showed up in his car, parked in the driveway, and wandered over, eventually dropping his long, skinny basketball hulk down on the grass.

"Let's go swimming at the pool," he suggested after regaining strength.

"Can't," Alan explained. "Waiting for Wigwam; may take him another hour or two to get here."

Newton grunted. Everybody knew that Wigwam was as reliable as a two-dollar fiddle, and that burro squared the result.

Both youths let pure silence take over until the far-off buzz of the San Francisco freeway reached them. Then out of sheer heat madness, Alan told Chuck about what happened this morning.

"Why did Becky want me to talk Walker into taking her to a movie?" he asked.

Newton sat bolt upright and stared unbelievingly at a fellow sophomore. "Whitlock," he said in his slow poet's voice, "I never thought you were this stupid. Sure, I knew you were dumb about some things, but — "

"What do you mean, stupid?" Alan inquired, sitting up too. A guy's pal could call him plenty of things, but nobody wanted to get in the public eyeball as being a stupe; it could prove too many teachers right and put a person into a foreign camp.

"About girls," Newton amended, "and — "

He couldn't complete the thought. From behind some trees came a blood-curdling howl. "Ahoy!" it hooted. "Avast there, fellow desert rats!"

Up on the hillside, Alan could see Wigwam near the corral. The guy waved his long, powerful gorilla arm. "Came by th' short cut, Whitlock," he yelled. "Mind if I tie my blue-ribbon burro near your horse?"

"Go ahead," Alan called. "Only don't put him inside the corral." Lately My Buddy hadn't cared for close burro companionship.

He and Newton waited while Wigwam got Xenophon some hay and filled an old rusty bucket with water. Then Tuttle panted down the slope.

"A guy provides for his burro before he thinks of his

88

own comfort, know that, guys? " he said, falling down full length beside his friends. " Man, it's real hot, so what have you chumps been doing to cool off? "

" Nothing," Alan said. If he told Wigwam about Becky, it would be the same as publishing the news in the *Lamagra Insider*.

" We were talking about women! " Newton had to babble.

Wigwam made a horrid face. " Look — " he gasped, " merely breathing today is a hard load. Newton, keep to pleasant stuff in these here poems you speak. You got a topic, pick something merely awful. Leave the ghastly for another day, please."

Newton shrugged. " The weak are always winnowed from the strong," he announced philosophically. " I was saying that Whitlock is stupid about women."

" And why shouldn't he be? " Wigwam grumbled. " Who isn't, except a couple of mad fools who enjoy self-delusions and stuff? "

" You say so, Wigwam," persisted Chuck, " but that doesn't make it essentially true, especially with women, because you may be an expert on burros, Tuttle, but there's still plenty you could learn about girls — although there may be possible transference. Now listen a second: Becky Linnell was — "

Wigwam shuddered so hard he woke up adjacent sparrows, probably with ground tremors. " For the love of heaven, Newton," he moaned, " I beg you not to discuss women and what do you do? You mention the name of that one woman who's the pure substance. Have some pity, please! " He clutched his forehead with a powerful paw and moaned some more.

" Yeah," Alan put in hastily. " Let it go, why don't you, Chuck? Let's talk about something we understand, like — " he searched a brain for a shred of know-how, " — like swimming, or — "

A cry came from Wigwam. " There y'go, Whitlock, mak-

89

ing things infinitely more complex. You even spin a New-
ton-type poem: wimmin in swimmin'." The guy rolled
over and beat clenched fists upon the warm turf. "All
right!" he sobbed. "Let's have it, Newton, if ya will! Give
us the coupe de glass!"

So naturally, that was what Chuck did; Alan had to turn
away in embarrassment while a pal told the works. "So
I've concluded that our companion, Whitlock, is pure
stupid!" the tall guy finished. "What do you think, Wigwam? Two heads are better than none."

Tuttle was silent a full ten seconds, which was itself
unique. Then he let out a pitiful little bleat. "Stupid!" he
yelped. "Why, Whitlock's practically a full genius when
it comes to women. He's like pure insane!"

A vast irritation mounted within Alan, compounded by
the heat and not being with a horse in mind and spirit.
"Cut it out, please," he growled ominously. "I'm in no
good mood for —"

"Look, stupid," Wigwam told him in a kindly voice,
"Becky Linnell wanted you to ask her yourself. Otherwise why did she mention that some youths who didn't
own cars were hesitant to ask a woman into the butterfly
life of movie and malt because they didn't know that some
women would cheerfully —"

"That's right," Newton interrupted. "Even a character
like Tuttle here, a burro expert, knows that much about
women, Alan. You missed your golden chance. A person
gets only so many chances like that in a whole lifetime. So
the first half he spends in fumbling rare opportunity, and
the last half in these solitary regrets —"

Wigwam was groaning his appreciation of so neat an
aphorism, but Alan scarcely heard. A chill like dry ice had
stabbed his spine. It was true; if Becky had meant Walker,
she wouldn't have talked about somebody who didn't have
a car. Why? Because that creamy creep definitely had
wheeled transportation, and an Austin Healey Sprite at
that. So —

90

Logic ground its inexorable circle in his head. Suddenly, he was on his feet and walking in a daze — like one of those somnambulists who hike around in their nutty sleep. His companions wondered where he was going, and so did he.

"Whitlock — " Wigwam hollered. "Come back! Don't take it so hard because me and Newton didn't mean no harm — "

He kept on traveling. In a minute he realized where he was headed — toward the phone, because here it was, in his hands. He called a number.

"Yes?" inquired this voice from the infinity of sweet outer space. "This is Becky — "

"This is Alan Whitlock. Would you go with me to — " He had to stop because he'd pushed ahead so aggressively he'd outrun any sensible words.

"Yes, Alan," she said in a shy tone. Girls got scared of a bold, forward youth. "Would I go with you to — "

"To see *Give a Man a Horse* — "

"Yes, to see *Give a Man a Horse* — "

"Tomorrow night?"

There was a pause while heartbeat thunder rumbled along the whispering wire and into his ears.

"Oh, I'd love to go," said Becky Linnell. "What ever made you think to ask me?"

It was probably mental telepathy that got him to do it, he realized later. They both wanted to go to this great horse movie and he'd had this mysterious inspiration to ask her. Maybe that was how it got to be with a guy and his shy woman.

The rest of the afternoon and all the next day he walked around on these candy clouds of ecstasy — right up until a couple of hours before he was supposed to stumble over to the Linnell house on shoes of feet and pick up Becky.

Then, as he was getting ready for three or four hours, cold reality set in. He *was* stupid when it came to women, only not in the common style Wigwam and Newton had claimed. His kind of stupid was about a hundred times worse.

The truth clouted him while he was looking at himself in the bathroom mirror and trying to create order from the chaos he had for a face. Sure, he'd been out with plenty of girls before, like Beulah Belt in his freshman year, for one. He'd escorted that siren of the sex to the Freshman Rocka-billy — which had been a sample of those girl-ask-boy fiascos. The affair had held its magic, all right, except that Miss Belt was a little on the hefty side, but a gorgeous creature, no doubt. The only tender word he'd had with that girl afterward was once when he'd told her hello two days before the year closed. Or it could have been good-by; he didn't remember; anyway, it was one of those subtle amenities.

Before that he'd been in the mode, naturally, following dictates of his generation, which were intended to abolish dictates of previous ones. In the seventh grade he'd gone steady the same as every other idiot in class. For one two-week period he'd really traveled the route, going steady with six different girls consecutively, and with two con-tiguously, using the highborn word.

In the eighth, romance had tapered off due to U.S. Con-stitution study up to as high as three hours a week. A per-son didn't have much left with that kind of madness, so he'd just gone steady with about a dozen girls in the whole year, most of those being the little lost loves that termi-nated right around Christmas.

But this was different; with Becky Linnell he couldn't play fast and loose the way he'd done in the good old days at grammar school. This, man, was love. He really liked that girl.

It had to be, from what he saw in the fatal glass — an image of a youth so young he was still wrestling the joy-bumps of life here and there. In smiles and other expres-sions all he had was one mouth and a couple of rows of teeth, some still showing that hint of orthodontia wire. There was a single nose, a couple of eyes, and about an inch of insipid hair growing around a mere head. That was all. It was asking quite a bit of a girl that she love something crass like that.

"Becky!" Alan breathed aloud, noting his one good quality; he had a healthy tongue color, but he didn't think that would interest the genuine princess of last year's sophomore class.

As he was dressing, he faced the final truth. By flinging himself this way into the frenzied social whirl they had in Lamagra — movies, malts, hamburgers, and the like — he had committed himself to laying out a sizable vein of his precious gold. He didn't really mind that; a Whitlock was a guy who could spend like a prince no matter what it cost in porridge or pelf. Look at all the pelf he had laid out for that horse without a backward glance! The trouble was that a person had only so much of the stuff, and beyond that was vile penury.

He'd been able to float a loan for this one night of bliss, but it was deficit financing. His dad had advanced a few dollars on future trash disposals over and above the call of duty.

But what of the morrow. "What?" he asked himself aloud. There was no answer.

Mr. Goulart might let him work four hours a day instead of three, but that wasn't likely. Even if it were, one more minute would get him because right now he was at his outermost gunk limits.

He might get another job; nowadays that was the way everyone lived, especially older men who had given in and gotten married. A man did his regular eight or ten hours at the normal job, and then after supper he whipped out to do the second task which helped him drag in all the opulent living, or, as the wily French called it, the *joie de vivre*. Another style was to have your wife work, but usually that happened later on when the shiny luster of romance had thinned down through the first layer of chrome.

If he and Becky were going to follow this endless round of the cinema, it might save trouble to get a job ushering. But that was unreal. In the first place, the Granada had quit using ushers right after television became the people's entertainment. Now a person bought his ticket and then stumbled around anywhere in the blackness. When he tripped he nearly always fell into an empty seat.

Alan discovered he'd gotten ready a little early, especially on daylight-saving time. He had to waste about an hour sitting around the home and listening to mood music. King Aztec caused trouble. The dog suddenly took a liking to him, probably because he was dressed in finery such as slacks and a coat woven mostly from Dacron. The King hung around, sniffing at shoes, until he got so tired of shoving him away that he locked him in Dorothea's room. So that girl had to run to her mother about cruelty to dumb dogs who belonged to other people.

Later, after supper, he told them good-by, saying: " So long," in this nonchalant voice. " I'll be in — "

He meant he'd be in early, but he didn't want to mention a time like midnight, because he'd hate to have to hang around outside for a couple of hours to make good his word.

" My! " his mother said, her eyes shining like Brazilian diamonds. " You look so grown up, and so handsome! " It was a fib, of course, but it gave a son spurious confidence for a minute.

The Linnell residence wasn't far — no more than a couple of miles. This was a fine evening for a walk, warm with a light breeze, and the moon would probably look even better later on when it got dark. Streets weren't crowded with pedestrians, which was all right; Alan hoped nobody he knew would see him dressed in this highborn style.

94

He hadn't gone more than a few blocks before he realized that he wasn't alone. As he passed a shaded place, a clump of willows spoke to him.

"Whitlock," the clump said, "you're a true sunburst of color. Man, you blaze a person's weary eyeballs!"

The clump turned out to be Wigwam, who was sitting there with Newton in his car. He had quite a conversation with them, because they drove along beside him in low gear for about a mile, giving the needed touch of last-minute advice. They let on how a necktie really set off the front aspect of a Whitlock, while the slash in a sports coat pointed up the great features of a guy's back. It was nice to know that a person had true friends behind him through thin and thick.

Finally he told them: "Get lost, you condor-vultures. Beat it — "

"So all right, pal, Wigwam said in sorrow. "We'll go; you already told us to fifty times. But remember this: You're on your own now. You're alone, Whitlock!"

They roared off and it turned out true. He was really alone. Ahead was the Linnell estate. Inside that house was skinflint Linnell, Becky's lovable old father.

Well, faint heart never took a woman to a fair movie. He swung up the steps with a bold stride and pushed the plastic button that set off the giant mandarin chimes within. Mrs. Linnell opened the door and after the customary informal chatchit a guy had with a girl's mother, Alan found himself seated in the living room.

Opposite him was Mr. Linnell. How a girl like Becky or even Mrs. Linnell could be related to him would make a good question to ask anthropology professors when he got to college. To Alan, skinflint Linnell had always looked as though he was trying to digest a can of corned beef from Argentina, tin and all. He'd supposed it to be an occupational pose, never before realizing that the man carried his work into the home.

They didn't converse too much, for which Alan was

thankful. Mr. Linnell merely wiggled bushy eyebrows into a more forbidding scowl and said, "Howrm!" In a way, that was a big idea when a guy took time to think it over.

He was watching the Friday-night fights, so Alan watched too: Buck McGurk versus Tex (Tornado) Valentine. The Tornado cut McGurk to pieces in five rounds, and Mr. Linnell seemed pleased. Later on, he figured it was because McGurk looked a lot like the average mortgagee around Lamagra. According to his dad, American could foreclose on a guy if he failed to lick the envelope's stamp just right for his next payment.

It was nice to know her dad intimately this way. At last Becky came down the stairs looking so beautiful Alan could almost forget he owned a pretty horse.

"You're walking?" Mr. Linnell grunted as they were leaving. His brows were up there getting acquainted with his haircut.

Alan flushed; it wasn't the usual glass coach a person needed to take out the town's Cinderella, he had to admit. "Yessir!" he said. "I —"

"At least you'll be safe in traffic then," her father finished. He sounded as if he didn't think Alan had too much know-how in crossing city streets even afoot.

They had a perfect evening together. On the way, Becky told him she knew he was a true horseman from the style My Buddy responded. Only a sure hand on the reins could bring about that light mouth and certain performance. A girl could know a boy by the kind of horse he owned, she claimed. No lie.

"You absolutely must enter him in the Gymkhana, Alan," she said as they neared the Granada box office. "He's so lovely and — and perfect. You'll do it, won't you?"

Who wouldn't for a neat girl like Becky, even though it meant that his horse would show the whole town and county what a rotten horseman he had for an owner!

"Sure I will," he told her in such a deep voice that his

96

tonsils got to vibrating backward, until he had to cough. "Wouldn't miss it."

The movie was the greatest, the most — except that the horse, Panamint Gold, was so much smarter than Stony Johnson that a guy wondered why the girl fell for him instead of the equine. Stony played his usual role, a simple cowpoke who was pure ignorant, although the fast gun in Tombstone. Six different times, Panamint Gold saved Stony's life — from drowning, by kicking a boulder down on a bad guy, and by two or three other superhorse deeds. Panamint Gold reminded Alan too much of My Buddy to make it a comfortable film to watch.

Anyway, with Becky sitting only about a foot away he could scarcely breathe, let alone keep his mind on the plot. Once while Panamint Gold was but a colt getting schooled by wiser wild horses on the old prairie, Becky waved her arms around at the same time that Alan was trying to pass her another sack of popcorn. Their hands touched, and even though she'd spilled refreshments, the spot burned with divine fire. All through Panamint Gold's interesting colthood, he felt that spot and it robbed the drama of some of its crazy punch. But at that, it was the most opulent horse movie he'd seen this year.

Afterward they stopped at The Straw Shack for malts and hamburgers, and sure enough, he learned that Becky had a healthy appetite. For one split second, he visualized again what kind of gold reserves this April love was going to demand, but he snuffed out that poltroon thought. A youth had to live for the now and not count the costs. In these times, people even bought cemetery lots on time because it kept down inflation and anchored the economy to solid ground.

Then who should walk in but Leroy, with Cynthia Ballard tagging along beside him merely to drink in his exotic masculine aura — to judge from the way Walker acted. He crowded Cynth into one of the rich plastic booths, fed a dozen dimes into the jukebox, and then ambled over to give a person's evening some sparkle.

"Hi, Becky," the guy rippled out across his gleaming teeth. "You too, Whitlock." Then he prattled on about what a great day he had brought the slumbering village of Lamagra, while Cynthia sat alone and Becky Linnell smiled.

Alan put on the suave display, pretending interest in malt alone, but of course he had to drag too deeply on the .32 caliber straws they had here and it made an awful sound of the pump at work, sumping.

"Ha!" Walker snorted. "Get your money's worth, if you must, Whitlock, but don't try to dig below the glass."

Becky giggled and April love did a nose dive in the snowbank. Yeah, Alan thought, give a man a horse.

"How'd you get down here, Becky?" Leroy sneered. "Your dad lend you his car, Whitlock? A gambler in every family."

April love suddenly got back into the sunshine. "We walked," Becky said for them both. "We like to, Leroy. Oh, riding around in your Snipe is fun, but so is walking beneath the lovely silver moon."

Walker's grin died hard, but everything in this world has to go, probably. "It's called a Sprite," he corrected with some difficulty in meshing throat gears. "Well, go ahead and have your mad heel-and-toe carousel, Whitlock. I'll take driving."

He hustled back to Cynthia, while on the jukebox "Lonely for You in a Crowd" howled forth like a pack of timber wolves trapped in a marble quarry.

Walking home together was a moment to remember always — although Alan realized that a girl could get so healthy it might be difficult to hike this way and appreciate the evening at the same time. Even this late it was still warm, and the clothes geniuses always had to cheapen their magic Dacron by putting in a whole mess of wool.

They didn't need to say much, because love was this

98

way. He was content to be silent at her side and listen to her tiny heels pounding the sidewalk. Besides, he had the creepy sensation that they were being followed at a discreet distance by a couple of guys in a rod. Once or twice he thought he saw a mechanical wraith duck back behind corners. It was probably imagination.

At last they stood on her porch in the witchery of the night, although the Linnell house was lighted up like the Point Piedras beacon, so that the moon had a tough time getting through. Through costly draperies within, muted notes of the late show reached them — a great serialized epic that Alan recognized as " Confidential Teacher." It told how this fine educator had rooted out subversive ideas being insinuated into the innocent minds of the junior high school mob.

Becky was as lovely as a naiad with the soft golden light suffused on her cheeks and with her eyes hidden in violet shadow. " I — I had a perfect time, Alan. I loved every minute of it."

Then she just stood there, with a funny little kind of smile on her lips, gentling them. She acted as if she expected him to do something unusual.

Untamed instincts stirred within Alan Whitlock and he recognized the fierce, aggressive man-instinct that ripped around in guys. Sure, it was taking advantage of a defenseless girl like Becky who was here without the protection of — whoever went around protecting her; skinflint Linnell, doubtless. But Alan didn't care.

" Will y-you g-go with me to — to — " He choked there; he couldn't go through with it.

" *Crazy Horse at Little Big Horn?* " Becky asked softly in a woman's sweet way. " Next week? "

" Yes," he said.

" Oh, I'd love to, Alan."

There was a silence; the moon seemed to brighten and the air grew fragrant with maybe hibiscus and heliotrope. Her blue eyes were deep, and tiny lights twinkled there.

99

For a second she worried him; a guy could be too aggressive and scare a shy girl like Becky.

" 'Night," he managed.

" Good night, Alan," she told him. " And thank you ever and ever so much for a lovely, lovely evening."

" G'night," he told her again. " I — "

But she was gone on the wing tips of a song, as Newton might say in his Edgar Allan Poe manner.

A moment later he was walking again past the shadowed willows. Out of one bunch came a spectral voice. " Whitlock," it said, " want a ride home or are you just going to go on walking — walking — in the crazy night? "

It turned out to be his faithful pals, Wigwam and Newton. They'd just happened to be cruising by.

" You are stupid! " Wigwam said. " About women, I mean."

" What do you infer? " Alan wanted to know.

But Tuttle wouldn't divulge any more, but instead merely whistled " Lips Are Meant to Be Kissed " the whole way home.

8:

IT WAS EARLY Sunday morning — or possibly late Saturday night — when Alan was awakened by a tapping on his door. He groaned a couple of times, then rolled over. " Who is it? " he asked.

" It's me — " somebody outside said, " or rather, it is I, your father. I want to find out — " The rest was too muffled to hear.

Alan sat up with difficulty, painfully aware that a person never really got broken in to Condorgas. Broken down would be a better way to describe the condition. Yet he was wide awake because of astonishment at who was up. Yesterday Mr. Whitlock had come home with a terrible case of what he insisted was old-fashioned Formosa Flu. The thought grabbed a son that his old dad was probably stumbling around the house in delirium.

Alan was sure now that he'd heard Mr. Whitlock saying: " I want to find out where's the water. Water! " The awful fever was probably boiling everything away.

He hurried over and flung open the door. Sure enough, it was his dad. The man's hair was standing up on end and he wore his heavy winter bathrobe to ward off the ninety-degree evening chill. A person was really sick when he looked like that.

" Dad! " Alan cried in consternation. " What's the trouble? Can I — "

" There's nothing the matter with me," replied Mr.

101

Whitlock, "except this infernal cold. But I do wish you'd please get up and find out what's the matter with that poor — that poor little horse."

He had pushed into the bedroom and now collapsed into a chair. His son came back and sat down on the edge of the rumpled bed. Sometimes the Formosa Flu got people like this, Alan knew. Last year at school, Bill Sudbunny III, a notable drip around school, had gotten it so bad that he'd ached in bones and muscles for one whole semester, especially in world history class. After that any sophomore who came down with the malady hadn't called it flu at all, but spoke of having been nailed by Sudbunny's Plague, until for a while it looked as if the name was going to catch on in such national medical journals as the women's magazines.

"Mind if I sit down?" Mr. Whitlock asked a little plaintively. "Just for a moment. I'm too exhausted to stand and talk at the same time."

"Sure, Dad," Alan told him warmly, repressing an impulse to suggest to a father that since it was the middle of the night, why stand and talk at all. Why not crawl back into bed and build strength?

"I can't sleep," his dad said weakly, as if reading minds. "That's why I came in here to ask you to please get out there and see if you can't quiet that poor, pitiable horse."

"Horse?" Alan exclaimed. "What horse?" He hadn't heard any horse around here — except the one who owned the place. Maybe his father meant that some stray horse had broken loose and was messing around the corral.

"My Buddy!" Mr. Whitlock replied.

Alan hurried over to the window. Outside nothing stirred; the hillside and the corral were lost in the blackness of night. "But, Dad," he said, "it's not even dawn yet. He doesn't get up until then."

"That's what you think," Mr. Whitlock sighed. "I envy you young people with your glowing health." He chuckled hollowly, finishing with a dry little cough. "You can

102

sleep through anything — earthquake, gore, Gehenna — "

"Gehenna? What's that, Dad?"

"Gehenna is — But never mind now," said Mr. Whitlock a bit sternly. "Gehenna can wait. The point is that your horse is fitful. He's been rapping on his stall all night and chuckling to himself in a most disagreeable manner. He's not right — "

How true! My Buddy wasn't right! Leave it to a guy's father to put the finger on the true trouble with a person's horse. Alan had thought of everything by now, but the idea that his faithful steed was a tiny bit crossed up in head from having too much horse sense had never occurred to him before. Even this early in the day — around two in the morning, as Alan judged — it made logic.

"He may be sick," Mr. Whitlock continued. "At least I am, and he hasn't allowed me a wink of sleep the whole night long. I won't ever be able to get up and support this — achoo! — this family if — "

"You're going to work, Dad? It's Sunday."

"Makes no difference — " Mr. Whitlock's voice trailed off, like that of a brave guy who knows when he's licked but has to get back into the fight just the same. "Get a flashlight and go out and — and bring your horse whatever nonsense he wants. Tell him to — "

"I can't — " Alan began, meaning My Buddy wouldn't tell him why he got amused at something in the middle of the night.

"Piffle — " said Mr. Whitlock, coughing again, "paffle! Of course you can; you know that horse like a brother. He — he likes you and you understand him. In a way, you and that horse are kindred " — more coughs — " spirits; or adolescents." He got up and weaved away on these unsteady footprints. At the door he said: "Keep him quiet a half hour. Or fifteen minutes. Maybe I can — " he yawned, " drop off, or — "

Alan watched his father disappear into shadows. Well, that was the way things were going with this family lately.

103

Mr. Whitlock had a definite case of Sudbunny's Plague, but he wasn't willing to accept.

He fumbled a pair of jeans on over his pajamas, located some sneakers that felt as though they were both for the left foot of someone else, and crept out into the night. He had the family flashlight, yanked from its magnetic moorings inside the broom closet, but he didn't turn it on except for a brief flicker or two to keep himself from falling over a garage.

He was sorry his father was so sick because back there at two o'clock in the morning he sensed that a rare moment had passed. His dad and he had just missed the one case of privacy they'd had in about a year. It had been a long time since Alan had yearned for the old-style father-son relations they'd lived through together back when he'd been a little freshman kid. In those nostalgic days, if he'd had a real problem like this one with My Buddy, he would have taken it straight to the wide shoulders of a true parent. He would have said, "You raised a no-good son, Dad — a guy too weak to master a light horse or even aspire toward that simple goal." Then he could have gone on to explain that rather than being a horse master he was a horse's bond servant instead. His dad might not have admired him for it, but he would have understood.

Not now. Alan sighed; the good old days were gone, probably forever. Now he had to work out stuff alone.

He began to recall a couple of adjectives his father had used, like "poor little" horse. For a while when My Buddy had first taken over, it had seemed to Alan that Mr. Whitlock wasn't entirely an ally of the equine. He had seemed to favor humans over horses. Once or twice he'd even said so. "Oh, let the boy finish his breakfast," he might announce. "Alice, it won't hurt that nag to wait a few minutes while Alan has another half dozen waffles."

In those far days of maybe a week ago, nobody would allow Mr. Whitlock to use harsh language like that in referring to My Buddy. "Don't you call him a 'nag,'
104

Daddy," Dorothea might say. "He's not a nag; he's fine, and — and noble. That's what he is. He's kind and generous the way fathers ought to be if they happened to be horses."

The whole picture had gotten obscured right there when Mr. Whitlock tried to explain to that girl what it would mean around Lamagra if she really did have that kind of father.

Yes, back there he had longed to blurt out the whole sorry story that My Buddy had arrived as a perfect horse and then bad handling had ruined him. His dad would have known the solution right away, because in olden times at Yreka he'd had plenty of experience denied to modern youths. Mr. Whitlock could have straightened out My Buddy's thinking and life around here would be happy and serene.

Now Alan guessed it was too late. Yesterday afternoon the situation had finally gotten out of hand entirely, or rather, out of seat. My Buddy was turning into a horse who was definitely not for a guy with an insecure seat, and no matter what he did, Alan had to admit that he had one of the most insecure.

What had the famous horseman said in the book? "It is the horse that has absolute confidence in himself that becomes the brilliant hunter." Well, now that My Buddy had decided to take up hunting and jumping as a career it proved that not even the most experienced handler could ever grasp the whole picture. The way Alan saw it, that palomino not only possessed absolute confidence; he had this positive horse thinking as well. It showed what could happen to somebody who began reaching for the stars without actually checking the gas in the spaceship.

Sure, Alan realized that the entire misunderstanding was his fault. In secret training out near the Salinas River, he'd encouraged My Buddy to jump a couple of ditches about a foot wide, which the horse did so well that he'd tried him over a six-inch log.

105

But did that mean a guy's horse had to go out and try for a record? Now My Buddy had decided to jump obstacles any time he felt like it. If he saw a fence low enough, he'd turn aside and jump it for fun. That was all right to keep practicing the Four Freedoms of horsedom, but it wasn't so good for a rider who wasn't with his horse, or if the fence happened to be keeping in somebody's good turkey ranch.

Yesterday afternoon, though, he'd gotten the real jolt. He'd ridden over toward Becky Linnell's place, keeping to back ways where there weren't any streets. He hoped he might see his woman to discuss their next magic date.

He was in luck; he did see her out near the Linnell horse barn across the open meadow. He'd ridden in that direction with quite a bit of confidence himself. There weren't any fences, ditches, logs, or anything in the field — only some grass stubble where hay had been mowed and baled last spring.

My Buddy went trotting across that field in perfect form, so Alan straightened up in the saddle with a flourish so that a person's girl could see what a neat horseman he was. When a rider couldn't count on anything else, he could always hope to make a good appearance.

That wasn't to be. As they neared the fence line of the Linnell property, Becky had turned and waved in that girlish style of women who happened to be dressed in their fancy, dancy Western finery — as if the dreamy eyeballs of all Texas were upon her.

Alan wanted to wave back the glad greeting, but just then he saw My Buddy's ears snap forward in a style he'd learned to recognize. It was how that horse got set to jump; he'd put his delicate, intellectual ears forward at twelve o'clock, focus on the target, bunch muscles, and then let fly. If a rider didn't go for barbed-wire puzzles too much, he got set right along with his horse.

Yet this one time, confusion set in. There wasn't any obstacle and it was fairly logical to question why My

106

Buddy was giving with the jump signals with nothing to leap. Also, a difference in general purpose complicated the maneuver. Alan wanted to appear easy in the saddle like Western chumps were expected to be — sort of as if he were part of his horse, as books described it. My Buddy wanted to get set for a jump which wasn't there. It was like what newspapers called " a conflict of interest."

Then the palomino jumped, and it was a while before Alan understood that a horse like My Buddy, who had plenty of imagination, could jump imaginary obstacles as easily as real ones. As it was, he'd gotten unstuck from the seat, not being able to visualize the same invisible fence, and he barely managed to hang on. He dismounted in front of Becky, red-faced with embarrassment.

" It's a trick I've been teaching him," Alan had explained. " He doesn't know it too well yet."

Meanwhile, My Buddy pawed the turf and nodded, well pleased with himself, and at that he was the world's champion imaginary obstacle jumper, Alan supposed. A champ had a right to be proud.

At first Becky had been surprised, claiming she'd never seen the trick before, not even on television. But later she admitted there had to be some innovations and probably jumping the imaginary obstacle course would become a regular event at rodeos and horse shows. There could be imaginary obstacle-jumping breeding stock to carry on the art. She wanted to try My Buddy on two or three imaginary jumps herself, but Alan wouldn't let her. He claimed it was too dangerous for a weak girl.

After that, he'd arranged about hiking her down to the movies, to the giant wide-screen spectacular filmed in Rome, Italy, which was titled *Crazy Horse at Little Big Horn*. He'd ridden off toward home, turning in the saddle to wave good-by.

Shortly afterward, My Buddy had gotten cured of imaginary obstacle-jumping, and that was what Alan wanted to talk over with his dad. He'd found out for sure that

107

the palomino wasn't too strong in brain in the usual style, no matter how sound he was of wind and straight of bone, well let down, and all that.

He'd taken a roundabout route home, working out the little kinks in horsemanship every inch of the way because Becky had made him promise again that he'd enter the junior rodeo. Details. The narrow dirt road he'd chosen was one that had been left over after Lamagra was laid out by wise old city planners. It wound lovingly through some nice hills and finally disappeared into the Salinas River, which may have been one reason it got abandoned. Still, it was a favorite with sophomores from clear back in grammar school because it ran along the edge of Lamagra Creek for a couple of miles and furnished easy access to trout and sucker fishery. Also, it passed beside Garson's Sand and Gravel Company where Mr. Garson could often be viewed filling his dump truck with a skip loader. A little beyond was a place that everyone in the know called " Garson's Pond " because Mr. Garson had shoveled it out in search of richer gravel deposits. People not in the know were usually a guy's parents.

Garson's Pond was a deep spot where the creek met the river. Water stood there eight or ten feet deep all summer long, whether the river dried up or not — which was always from June onward. If a person didn't mind a lot of green scum and polliwogs, plus some other unclassified stuff, it made a great arena to practice swimming before you had your Australian crawl fit for pool or shore. Another feature was that it always became screened from public view by a thin hedge of natural bush and flower growing along the road. Alan regarded the place as a pleasant refuge from life's mad whirl, although it was a couple of years since he'd been there. As a sophomore grew older, he began to agree with his mother. Polliwogs and green scum in pants cuffs didn't help automatic washer-drier combinations achieve the smooth operation of their silky magic brains.

108

"Easy! Easy!" he told My Buddy as they began to pass the place. "This is where I used to hang out when I was a kid." Talk with your horse, they said. Well, Alan was willing to tell him everything.

My Buddy had nodded and begun to go on by. Right then, a jack rabbit or perhaps a covey of quail on the opposite side of the road had decided to take off with plenty of racket that could frighten a horse. It was either that or he'd decided to jump another unseen fence.

"Whoa! Whoa!" Alan had yelled, pulling up hard.

It didn't do any good because when that horse set his unique brain to an idea he was as bad as a juvenile delinquent. He went ahead and did it whether you liked him to or not.

My Buddy jumped, not stopping to count costs or look before he leaped. This time, naturally, it had to be his finest effort. He sailed over the line of bushes. Right when he reached the apex of his jump he saw what lay ahead.

Alan heard this hysterical clarion, and if neighbors thought the wild scream of the inland stallion was bad, they should have heard My Buddy airborne over Garson's Pond. It was enough to freeze lizard blood.

Instantly afterward, Alan knew why his faithful horse had yelled in that style. He didn't like water too well and for a very sensible reason. In every movie a guy saw, horses were always pulling riders out of rivers, or fording the raging stream to get the doc to some dying cowboy. It could be true with the general run of horseflesh.

Also, this was the first true bellyflop by a horse Alan had ever witnessed and it was interesting, but not so much up this close. There was this tremendous splash, and the next thing a guy knew he was swimming with one hand, trying to strike out for shore by reflex action and getting nowhere.

Logic compelled him to look around to find out what was holding back his other hand. He saw it still gripping the leather with the reins going straight down into Garson's

109

Pond. My Buddy was nowhere in sight, and at first Alan had thought a smart horse like that would have swum out of there and bolted for dry ground.

Down below, Garson's Pond was a boiling vortex with gobs of scum erupting from the depths amidst practically pure polliwogs through the first six inches of surface.

"Well, what do you know!" Alan had to exclaim as he learned one more chunk of horse lore about My Buddy.

It was that which he'd wanted to tell his fine old dad.

My Buddy couldn't swim!

He was probably a desert horse or something, palominos having a lot of Arabian stock in them. Maybe he'd never seen water out of a pail before in his whole life.

One good thing, it meant that maybe that horse had extrasensory perception, because all that imaginary jumping practice came in handy now. The next second, the equine's head broke through polliwogs while he took in a vast bundle of air, after blowing out water like a sounding narwhal.

Then he went down again.

Alan had gotten ready to dive after him before his two more trips to the surface got used up. It was going to be a little difficult to bring in a light horse by tenderfoot Boy Scout swimming safety methods, but he had to try.

He'd found out what My Buddy was doing and it made a lot of sense: he was holding his breath under water and jumping imaginary obstacles. After four or five, he hit a sandy bottom and both of them crawled out on the bank.

Artificial respiration was going to have to be by the old-fashioned Schaefer method instead of by blowing into My Buddy's mouth, Alan knew. But it turned out that his horse was all right; he merely wanted to get gone from there and his master had a little trouble catching him.

He'd walked him until the horse was dry and then had ridden the rest of the way home, coming in from the rear so that neither Dorothea nor his mother could see. Then he'd spent the remainder of the day cleaning up: first the actual horse; then the saddle and bridle, while the animal stood around eating. One good result was that bellyflopping into Garson's Pond had cured My Buddy of jumping. Since then he hadn't jumped once.

It was probably a clue to the secret of accomplishing the rest of training for the rodeo and stuff, but Alan wasn't too sure he wanted a responsive horse that much.

He reached the corral, but it wasn't until he was inside, that he learned what his father had been talking about. He heard this eerie tapping on wood, followed by the low chuckle.

A chill swept down Alan's spine as he snapped on the flashlight. My Buddy was there, scrounging in the feedbox. He looked around, full into the circle of illumination. It happened again. First he banged the stall rhythmically with his muzzle; then he chuckled.

" It's — " Alan hesitated over the dread name. " It's Sudbunny's! "

Although the night air was balmy, he got out the stable sheet hastily, buckling it over the front legs first. Next he checked water and spread fresh hay around on the floor of the stall, getting it from the new bales under the tarp outside the corral. He'd had to lay in another half ton just last Tuesday, which by good luck happened to be Goulart's payday. By borrowing four more dollars from his mother, he'd had enough money.

After that, he petted his horse gently and listened a while to his chest, becoming more and more reassured. If it were really Sudbunny's, a guy's breathing sounded like a wind tunnel for helicopters, and it should be even worse with a thousand-pound horse.

" I hope you're not sick," he whispered. " I'd never forgive myself for letting you fall into Garson's Pond, old pal. Please — don't get Sudbunny's! " Horses could catch a million other diseases, like bots, roundworms, colic, sleeping sickness, and so forth. But none of those would be half so bad as what he feared.

My Buddy put his nose around and nuzzled Alan, trying to say that even if he did get Sudbunny's, he was going to be brave. There in the whispering night with the soft sounds of wild creatures moving around unseen — such as deer coming up to swipe hay, foxes, skunks — all that — a boy and his horse stood in this lonely togetherness for about an hour.

The horse hadn't coughed again, and since he was almost asleep anyway, Alan gave My Buddy a measure of grain, picked his careful way back to the house, and went to bed.

He'd just fallen asleep when the knock on his door roused him again. Sure enough, it was Mr. Whitlock.

"Alan," said the man with a sort of tremor in his voice, "not that I blame you, but why don't you go out and help your poor little horse as I told you to do some time ago. He's rapping on his stall even more now; he's chuckling — "

"But, Dad — " Alan whispered, "I did go."

His father coughed clear down to the shoe rack. Sudbunny's! Here in the house; out there! They'd caught it from each other, maybe; either his dad had caught it from the horse, or My Buddy had caught it from — No matter! He let it go now that the damage was done.

While Mr. Whitlock went back to bed, Alan found his old Boy Scout forest-green sleeping bag in a closet. He put that under his arm and went back to the corral. With a faithful master nearby, My Buddy found a lot of courage to go on. He didn't rap on the stall or chuckle during the rest of the night — although Alan had trouble getting any sleep.

His dad's bedroom faced this way and the man coughed something fierce all night long, every minute on the minute. It was nerve-racking for a son to hear his father giving in to Sudbunny's without a battle.

Late in the morning, Wigwam and Joe Nunez came over, riding Xenophon by turns. Alan was still out by the corral, although My Buddy had been healthy as a horse for hours.

"Hi, man," Wigwam yelled. "Want to go swimming before you go to work and earn all that filthy money you're hoarding?"

"No, thanks," Alan told him.

Just then, My Buddy looked around and saw Xenophon tied too close to his stall.

Joe had something interesting to say. "Want another job at the Lamagra Bowl?" he asked. "I'm working there now, Whitlock; it's recreational. Mr. Hawkins needs another pin boy and Wigwam says he don't want the money that bad."

"I like to be free," Tuttle explained. "I don't need much; only air, clean, cool water, home cooking, and my allowance. I'm not a moneygrubber, guys, the way —" He stopped. He was staring hard into the stall.

Alan and Joe followed Wigwam's hypnotized gaze. "That horse —" the guy said, "is putting the hex eyeball on my burro, or something."

At that precise point My Buddy coughed — a great hacking hollow sound that made Xenophon jump like an elk who'd learned that the city hunters were coming and nothing with horns would be safe.

"Maybe it's TB," Joe Nunez said in a hushed voice. "My uncle down in San Diego knows plenty about horses, and he told me —"

"It's worse than that," Wigwam said professionally. "Look at his ears turned back that way, and — Guys, Alan's horse has got a clear case of Sudbunny's Plague!"

9:

ALAN'S CONFUSION about his horse was by now complete; he didn't understand him at all and never would. Wigwam and Joe had hardly left the yard when My Buddy recovered lost health.

" — got the same thing," Wigwam had said, speaking of a palomino who had lived up in Carleton. " Owner — guy by the name of Dopey, or maybe it was Doheny — anyway, this guy didn't — " He left it there.

" What happened? " Joe had asked. " My uncle down in San Diego did the same thing, and he — "

Wigwam gave him a pitying stare. " Look, Nunez," he'd said, " a guy's uncle isn't the same as his palomino horse, try to understand that, will you? Whitlock, next time get yourself a hardy burro. Library is full of horse-disease books. You ever find one about burro sickness? No! "

My Buddy had coughed again while cold fear gripped Alan. " What happened to Mr. Doheny's palomino? " he'd asked.

Wigwam tried to look brave. He made a slicing motion across his throat latch. " I'm not sure," he'd choked, " but — Well, that there palomino isn't around any more. Last time I saw Mr. Dope he was in the Farmers' Alliance, pricing John Deere tractors."

A vision of one defunct palomino taking wing to the happy jumping grounds caught at Alan's heart. " Wow! " he whispered. " That bad."

114

"I guess!" Wigwam had told him cheerfully. "Well, gotta get on th' trail. C'mon, Xenophon. Whitlock, a burro can stand out all night in the blizzard's raging sleet without coughing. Likes it. Gives him a change of weather."

The two pals had taken off, riding double on a cast-iron burro who could endure the desert's blazing sun and the blizzard's blast without a murmur. At that, Xenophon hadn't accepted carrying both Wigwam and Joe too well. He'd practically kicked down the fence trying to unhorse those two guys, but in time he'd laid back his long ears and trudged off at a full one mile per hour.

Watching the burro go, My Buddy had coughed twice in the direction of travel, but after that he'd stopped. He'd seemed solid as a nut.

Nevertheless, Alan had decided not to work him for a few days, which had been difficult to explain to Dorothea. With Mr. Whitlock coughing around the house constantly and getting up from the table to go somewhere to sneeze, a son didn't think it wise to dwell on horse infirmities. It might make the common cold seem too big for one man.

"My Buddy's got a mild case of Sudbunny's, is all," he'd tried to explain to his sister in private.

"He has not," Dorothea had insisted later. "He hasn't got anything, Mother. I looked it up in the horse book and there isn't any such disease as Sudbunny's. Alan's making that up because he's selfish. Make him stop being selfish, Mother."

Mrs. Whitlock had said she couldn't retrain a son; there was no turning back now. All a mother could do was hope for the best.

Alan kept My Buddy warm, dry, and fed — which wasn't too hard. Each afternoon when he got home from Condorgas, aching from crest to fetlock, he went out and gave a sick horse light exercise. Not once in the whole time did the palomino feel the cruel snaffle bit or the crushing weight of the saddle upon his poor, tired back.

115

To make good use of the time, Alan set up some boxes and stuff in the adjoining field and led the horse through a turn that was something like the barrel race. My Buddy would circle close to all the obstacles as though he'd been walking the barrel race for life.

It was the same in figure eights; the palomino turned those with the precision and grace of a Russian ballet dancer and seemed to like it. What was even better, he didn't cough or sneeze the whole time, nor did Mr. Whitlock complain again that a horse was rapping and chuckling. Alan's father got well fast, and three days later he was going around telling people he never felt better in his life — which showed a person how awful his dad had been. Well, it meant that the ominous threat was over. A gentle hand, a kindly thought, plus hourly care from a considerate master, were winning after all, both with a dad and a horse.

After witnessing that *Crazy Horse* epic, Alan had asked Becky to ride over hill and dale sometime. She'd accepted and that date was today.

As for the movie, its main excitement was how they'd gotten about one million Italian extras to look like Sioux Indians. They were the most bloodthirsty redskins in Alan's recollection. He guessed it proved that science could do anything it wanted these days.

In one unforgettable scene, he'd thought he recognized the Roman Colosseum, and that was true, only it was this mirage the thirst-mad U.S. cavalrymen were seeing. When the vengeance of the tribe struck, Chief Crazy Horse gave the cavalrymen a drink of cool, cool water before he scalped them. It proved that Italian Indians were a lot kinder than regular Sioux.

The afternoon presented a dreamy prospect of a Western man and his woman out riding together — she in her bell-bottomed pants of peacock blue, silvery embroidered shirt, and genuine Dawnhay hat. Her black filly would be fitted out with the nineteen-pound Waxwing saddle and a

116

German silver bridle ornamented to make a lovely sight. And he and My Buddy? Well, they'd be there too — providing the palomino was willing.

Right now he was heading for the corral. To make his mount feel confident again, Alan approached with music. He began whistling a late tune, a catchy number called "The Battle of Berlin."

Rather than having the good effect, it seemed to get My Buddy off on the wrong hoof. As soon as Alan took down the bridle from its hook on the wall, the horse backed off a couple of steps and stood there shivering his hide.

"Easy, boy," Alan said. "Ee-a-sy; take it slow, pal. We're going for a nice ride this afternoon."

He held up the bridle in his left hand so that horse could see he wasn't concealing anything. Meanwhile he stroked My Buddy's neck. He sure had a fine neck; judging by neck alone this equine was the best of the herd.

His delicate ears were forward; they twitched back; then forward again. Alan worked his hand upward and raised the bridle while the animal opened his mouth dutifully at touch. The bit slid between his young teeth easily. With his free right hand, the master secured the chin strap so it was loose and comfortable as always.

Then it happened! My Buddy coughed deep down, with plenty of horsepower.

"Now, why did you have to go and do that?" Alan asked reproachfully.

Answering, that horse swished his white tail around and looked mighty sorry, while he snorted deeply and shuddered his burnished golden hide again. Finally he subsided.

One cough didn't mean much, Alan reassured himself. He'd heard most other horses cough occasionally and they seemed to do it in the manner of humans in an auditorium. For kicks. Also baboons did plenty of coughing — perfectly healthy baboons out in the veldt.

117

He waited to see if the sickness got worse, but My Buddy looked fine, so he went for the saddle, the old-style forty-pound job that felt as if it weighed a hundred. This he set outside where his horse could take a long look at it. Then Alan found a clean saddle blanket he'd washed recently.

A moment later he lugged the saddle over and lifted it, expecting My Buddy to shy. Apparently, bellyflopping in Garson's Pond had cured him of that too. He stood perfectly still as the saddle settled on his back in the center of the blanket. Alan had to blink from surprise; now if he could cinch up, this would be the perfect day.

He reached under the palomino, watching for hoofs all the time. There was nothing like having a light horse stand on a guy's foot just because he'd gotten distracted over some detail. But he was able to grab the cinch at once and pull it up with an extra snug ounce.

My Buddy tried to look at the saddle that was shining from saddle soap with the aprons soft and pliable. " It's all right, pal," Alan whispered. " We're set now, and — "

The horse had sucked in chest and belly; then came the sneeze, deep and wide, followed by a rumbling of horse nostrils, which could be a new event in the junior rodeo called " Prolonged Horse Snort."

" Hey! " Alan gasped. Anything that could sneeze this way had Sudbunny's Plague for sure. He waited; maybe it was only an allergy, like hay fever. It had been days since the palomino had sneezed at all, and —

My Buddy sneezed a second time; then a third.

For a couple of minutes, Alan debated going in the house and calling Becky that the ride was off. But he'd promised, and a Whitlock kept his word.

On trial, he took My Buddy out in the field and walked him around the barrel race course a couple of times. The horse perked up and became almost frisky, so Alan decided to chance it. Still, he made a couple of promises to a pal.

118

"We'll just walk," he said. "No trotting; no galloping!"

Even walking it seemed that My Buddy couldn't make it in one or two steep places. Alan kept remembering a book he'd read named *The Horse Appeaser* or something. It was about the good old days when there were twenty-seven million horses in America and not many people, so everybody owned a team.

These horse appeasers went around showing people how to manage their transportation. The method they used was pure kindness; the guy would pitch this horse down with a sort of rope come-along tied to hoofs. Or else he'd tie the animal's head to its tail and let him spin until he dropped over in a dizzy spell. The treatment was absolutely painless, the book said, and the horse got rewarded with a nice carrot. It probably helped the carrot industry a lot.

It had been a comfort to Alan because it proved that practically everybody in America had been a lousy horseman except these two or three guys. Afterward the bicycle had come in for women and the gasoline engine for men. It showed why an occasional no-good horseman showed up in modern times.

For instance, he felt cruel for making his poor weak horse walk up a hill carrying a person, so on one fairly steep incline he dismounted and led My Buddy. Except for being about an hour late, they made it fine. Becky was in the meadow riding Miss Moonfire this way and that and peering into likely bushes.

"I've been looking for you," she said. "I thought you weren't ever coming."

"Goofed on the time," Alan fibbed. He didn't want Becky to know he was the sort of unscrupulous person who would ride a sick horse even by leading him. Probably he should have carried My Buddy here on youthback, but he had to admit it wouldn't have been romantic.

"While I was waiting I've been practicing reining and

119

a few figure eights. Miss Moonfire and I won second in those events last year," she said proudly.

"You'll take first this year," Alan told her.

"Not with My Buddy in the competition," Becky came back. "He's sure to place."

Alan swallowed hard and nodded. He and his horse were going to place in the Junior Gymkhana, no doubt about it. But he didn't want to tell his woman where. Somebody had to be last or people didn't have a show.

"Sure he will; sure he will," he agreed with that bold confidence a horseman learns by hanging around horses night and day.

Becky's black filly was gnawing grass, so she leaned over to pat her giant neck. "Before we ride, Alan," she said, "let's try a couple of figure eights right now. I'll ride a few and you watch me for points and form; then you ride and I'll coach."

His brain moved with lightning precision. Miss Moonfire would do perfect figure eights. When he followed on My Buddy, the palomino would probably decide that a figure four was close enough this afternoon. Or maybe he'd settle for a plain zero. "It's getting late; maybe we should ride first and — practice later?"

"Mmm!" she mused, glancing at the sun, which was at two o'clock. "I suppose so. Well, let's ride just one. Please, Alan." She was smiling in her winsome style. What man could refuse?

Miss Moonfire showed marvelous technique while Alan and My Buddy watched. He had his eyes on his girl so tightly that he didn't notice how his horse's fine head rose and the nostrils flared.

"How'd we do?" Becky asked when she came trotting back.

"Great!" he said truthfully. "You were so good that I don't think we can — "

He couldn't finish. My Buddy took out past the black

120

filly and into the field. He went prancing along with little short steps while his head was held high.

"C'mon, pal," Alan said, reining properly. "As long as we're on display do a figure eight for luck."

They were already circling and crossing. A moment later they came out of whatever they'd done. Only My Buddy knew.

When he reached Becky's side again, Alan noticed she was looking away — probably from embarrassment in seeing that style figure eight. It took a while to grasp new ideas.

"Ha! Ha!" he said with a sickly grin, giving the light touch because he might as well try to pass this off as a joke: "We're the regular junior rodeo clowns, aren't we, Becky? The pure buffoons on horseback!"

She turned her lovely blue eyes full upon them. "Alan Whitlock," she said severely, "I don't think you should talk like that. Maybe it's your business if you want to run yourself down in front of everybody, but it isn't fair to a horse like My Buddy!" She picked up her reins. "We'd better ride now."

The first word she spoke after that was at the foot of a long hill. "Alan," she told him crossly, "if you must show off, I — I th-think I'll have to turn around and go home. I won't take your kind of chances with Miss Moonfire."

He knew what she meant. From having to drag My Buddy up this hill on foot, now he'd decided to take his head, so to speak, although Alan hadn't really offered it. "Whoa, boy!" he'd whispered, reining in hard. "Whoa!" Even so, the palomino persisted in dancing the whole road, first right, then left, until Miss Moonfire had naturally become nervous.

It turned out to be a real ride, but there wasn't too much social interplay about it. Alan spent the whole time checking his horse, turning him so Becky wouldn't decide to go home. When they returned he was worn out from horsemanship.

"It was a lot of fun," Becky told him. "We'll have to do this again."

"Sure," he told her. Sometime in a couple of years.

"I just love My Buddy," Becky said with her voice like the west wind. "I almost wish he were my horse, although I love Miss Moonfire too."

"I'll —"

Alan stopped just in time. He'd almost offered to give his valiant steed to his girl, but he couldn't do that of course.

"— be seeing you," he finished. It made logic because My Buddy had already decided it was about time to clamp on the old feed bag.

They were moving off, so he turned around in the saddle. She was still sitting there on nice, calm Miss Moonfire and both of them wore these quizzical expressions.

"You don't need to be so abrupt with me, Alan Whitlock!" she suddenly cried. "If you didn't want to go riding, you could have said so, and — Oh! You!"

He couldn't explain. "'By!'" he waved to her. He had to yell it fairly loud because of distance and it must have carried because he saw skinflint Linnell come busting out of their back door, waving arms.

As soon as they had topped the rise, My Buddy dropped from a smart gait to a slow drag and then dragged it all the way home.

Reaching his yard, Alan saw that he had company. Newton was there, sitting in his roadster.

A guy could envy that tall sophomore. The little car didn't have a brain of its own to decide details for the driver. If a person slid under that wheel and stepped on the accelerator only so far, it traveled at his pace. A person wouldn't have to walk it home to cool the engine, and he could put it into the garage at night and polish the finish a week from Sunday if he wanted to.

Maybe that was the real trouble with him and My Buddy after all. If a youth had the mechanical brain, probably a horse knew it and went ahead with his own animal-type thinking. Somebody had to make decisions when a horse and rider got out on the trail, and if a rider couldn't then a smart horse would, probably.

Newton didn't hang around long; he got bored with watching Alan sponge and comb the palomino.

"Got important business," he said. "Thought you might like to drag town a while. But you and I are drifting apart, Whitlock. Since you got a horse, you've changed. I used to think you liked cars."

"I do," Alan replied, trying to turn away for a second to talk with a friendly youth. But My Buddy shifted feet around so impatiently that he had to go back to the work.

"Not so you'd notice it," Newton returned. "Every time I come here lately you're petting that horse. Sure, I like horses; they're alive; they're warm-blooded. But they still aren't a rod and a rod is necessary in this age and day. I guess you're too hungry for a horse's affection to want a car."

"No — " Alan said, scrubbing vigorously with the damp sponge and drying right behind it with salt sacks. "I — "

My Buddy pressed in, asking for more sponge on his back.

"Some guys are nature lovers," Newton said a little wistfully. "I guess I'm cold. Maybe it's heresy, but I like the automobile — that good old reciprocating internal-combustion engine. I think the car was a good invention even though it did almost destroy the horse."

"So do — " Alan began, but My Buddy began to swish his tail around fast because a couple of flies had heard the good news. That horse wanted his stable sheet on him right now.

"So long, pal," Newton said, moving away.

"So — "

But the roadster's starter was already spinning over. The engine caught, roared to life, and backed out. Well, there went friendship, Alan thought. He was stuck with this beautiful love he had for My Buddy; they were here

123

together — one lonesome guy and his affectionate palomino.

At least after today he knew that his fears were groundless. That horse didn't have Sudbunny's Plague. No horse could who was so spirited and alert when they'd been riding with Becky and Miss Moonfire. Why, that comfortable animal in the stall was the picture of —

My Buddy scrounging the last of his grain in a peculiar style. He gave the salt lick a couple of swipes, took one more drink of water, and then leaned against the wall and began to tap.

"Chunk! Chunk!" went the tapping. Then he coughed!

It was a hollow, sick sound from far back in whatever hidden cough center a horse had in head. He looked around until his thin-lidded eyes met Alan's. There was reproach in that baleful stare that went all through a guy. It seemed to say that a palomino was bad off who had a cruel master — a guy who'd insisted on booting a horse over hill and dale on a warm day like this. A miserable day — probably the last in life for a self-sacrificing equine who was well let down.

10:

To ALAN, Dr. Bison didn't look too much like a real
doctor, but he had a good reputation in the county, particularly for curing sick cats and cows. He was a square-
shaped man, with powerful arms and hands, and small
piercing eyes that stabbed right through you and sized up
the sick animal in a guy.

The doc had driven here in an old GMC station wagon,
and after a few preliminaries about the patient, had gone
to work. He was still in My Buddy's stall while Alan stood
nearby awaiting the verdict.

Around home there had been quite a debate about
whether to call the doctor. Mr. Whitlock had looked the
horse over several times recently.

"He has a slight cold," he'd announced, "but it isn't
anything serious. A horse can have a minor cold just like
anyone else."

"I don't think you should minimize the problem," Mrs.
Whitlock had put in. "We can't afford to run any risks
with — with Alan's pet!"

Dorothea had felt the same way only more so, but she
didn't interrupt with opinions while her parents were
talking.

In the end it turned out that Alan's mother knew best
from taking care of sick children time after time. Even Mr.
Whitlock had to agree. "At least," he'd said, "it'll end this
argument. No, of course I'm not a veterinarian, Alice. I

simply thought we could wait a day or so longer, and — But no matter. Alan, you'd best summon Dr. Bison."

At first the vet had moved cautiously around the stall, which proved he was a true horseman. Now he was still cautious, which must prove something else. My Buddy had behaved perfectly so far. He'd acted as if he enjoyed being poked and prodded. Revealing personal secrets like whether his back teeth needed floating seemed good sport to that horse.

"Ther-e-e-e-e, boy!" Dr. Bison kept saying. "Eas-sy-sy-sy! Easy now-w-w-w, boy-y-y!" He talked to animals too, but a veterinarian probably knew the language.

Right now he came hurrying out of the stall to a bag he'd carried with him and set down outside.

"Is there anything —" Alan began.

"Just a minute," Dr. Bison snapped. "I want to give this horse a shot while he's quiet."

He took out a monster syringe with a needle as big as a crochet hook. Alan had to wince just from looking at it. The doctor stuck the hook through the rubber top of a bottle of white, fluid, sucked in deeply with the plunger, and then went back into the stall.

Alan held his breath. When that syringe got jabbed into My Buddy's muscle and bone, the stall roof would probably come off. But nothing happened, not even a horse snort. In another minute, the vet was back putting the syringe away.

Carrying his satchel, the man stood up. He met Alan's questioning glance with that disconcerting zoo-stare of his. "I gave him a little penicillin as a precautionary measure," he said.

"Has he got —" Alan almost said Sudbunny's Plague, but checked himself. The scourge hadn't been recognized by veterinary science either.

"Went over him completely," the doctor continued. "Can't find a thing wrong with him except that he *may* have a cold, but as far as I can tell it's slight. Does have a

126

faint wheeze in his chest, but — "

"That's what my dad — "

The doctor peered far off into the circling hills. Up there, probably, were wild animals, a lot of whom were sick today. But could they call a kindly veterinarian when they wanted one? No.

"Your horse is in reasonably good shape," the doctor went on. "Perhaps you've been feeding him too rich a diet. For the next few days give him less grain and more roughage — hay, and so on."

"Yes, sir."

"Light feeding and light work," the vet finished. "I'm sure he'll be himself in a few days. Call me if he seems worse."

Alan noticed that My Buddy shivered when the doctor mentioned work, but he didn't say anything; instead he watched the man make his way back to the car.

It was an immense relief to learn there was nothing wrong with a guy's horse. He went into the stall and stood there a while with the patient, stroking his shoulder gently and talking kind words.

He looked for the wound the vet's horror weapon had probably made, but he could find nothing, although My Buddy's hide shivered a couple of times during the search. The animal glanced around and nuzzled him before returning to his new diet full of good hay.

It suddenly occurred to Alan that his sixteenth birthday wasn't so far off, which was a strange thought to have while nursing an ill equine. Here in California, sixteen was the time the law let a person get a driver's license; then all a guy needed was a car to put his life on wheels and be in the mode.

He remembered that his mother had called My Buddy a pet. That was all a hard-working horse got to be these days — unless he was part of the actual working equipment of a ranch. At that most ranch labor was done by tractor, and cowmen even went out to inspect the herds in a jeep.

127

Only occasionally was a horse necessary — for rounding up strays in the steep hills, or during spring branding.

Alan felt deep compassion and identification with the palomino. He was merely trying to get along, do his share of the work, catch his quota of the common cold, and have a few good friends in a world that didn't need him too much.

He had to face it: the heyday of the horse was over. Now, with millions of cars around and everybody getting ready to blast off into outer space, there wasn't room left for the wild untrammeled herd. So an honest horse had to be a pet if he wanted to survive, get boxed into a box stall until he got sick and needed a vet to jab him with a needle the size of a tenpenny nail. That was life.

"I'm sorry!" Alan said, apologizing for what the world did to a good horse. "I really am, pal."

An impulse seized him to turn My Buddy loose to run free among the deer and the — He'd almost said "antelope," but there hadn't been a real antelope around here since a traveling circus hit town. Still, he caught a vision of this gorgeous, strong, noble horse of his running wild and happy out there — battling the wily mountain lion, kicking the starch out of the dangerous black bear, feeding in the quiet, hidden meadows of the Coast Ranges, and drinking the sparkling water from a secret spring.

He sighed; he couldn't do that. They both had to be realistic. The truth was that even a horse had to be a pawn of civilization the same as a sophomore youth who worked at Condorgas to bring in the daily hay and call the vet.

"Probably neither of us will ever be free," he whispered. "We'll have to clank along in the crazy chains for life."

"Alan!" somebody called from the house.

One lone philosopher of the tragedy of the passing horse stuck his head out of the stall. He saw Dorothea.

"Yeah!" he hollered to her. "What is it?"

"Telephone! Somebody wants you on the telephone."

"Who does?"

128

"Some girl!" Dorothea screeched. "I THINK IT'S BECKY LINNELL!"

His cheeks burned; this was another example of what they did to guys and horses. They screamed out a name like Becky's and turned something sacred into common property.

"All right, all right," he said. "I'm coming."

Dorothea said something else that was lost in the banging of the screen door. Well, by now the whole neighborhood knew Alan's gossamer woman was on the phone. Old man Fegley would probably come out and stare over in this direction to ask why some neat girl like Becky Linnell would call up a creep like him.

As he hurried toward the house, he began to doubt that it was Becky at all. A shy woman like her didn't go around seeking out a youth by telephone; he had to seek her. It was Wigwam or Newton wanting some little thing, and saying it was Becky Linnell could be Dorothea's hilarious sense of humor. A joke like that could panic a freshman; they were hysterical to begin with.

He was out of breath when he reached the phone. "Hi, Wigwam, or — " he gasped.

It was Becky after all. "Dr. Bison stopped here this morning to check Miss Moonfire's shoes," she said in her lustrous, glamour-strewn voice. "He told me he was on his way to visit My Buddy. Oh, Alan, how is he?"

For an instant he was so overcome by astonishment and emotion he couldn't answer; besides, he had to pick right words to describe that equine's precarious condition. But it was pretty fine of Becky; most women wouldn't think of asking how a person's horse was getting along. They were too concerned with the hustle and bustle of being just girls.

"He has a cold, is all," he was able to tell her. "That's what I figured all along, but to be on the safe side I called the vet."

"You never can be too sure!" Becky agreed. "Why,

129

once Miss Moonfire caught colic, and I've never been so frightened in all my life."

It turned out that every girl in the Pony Belles had faced the same grim ordeal of a horse poised precariously on the knife-edge of sickness. Becky knew the names of more horse diseases than they had horses in this town, and she sort of gave him the idea that any one of them could strike without warning and lay a guy's steed lower than a snake's uncle.

" By the way, Alan," she said after she'd finished with disease. " There's a new shipment of books in the library. They got a few good ones this time instead of those young adult things about youth's problems. Ugh! I've been begging Miss Derring to order them. One is *Buckskin Holiday* — it's had wonderful reviews. Another is *Mustang Stallion's Wisdom,* and the last is *Wild Horse Canyon,* which is real literature. It's about how Steve Bailey, the hero, and his skewbald stallion capture these crooks from outer space. I'm going down this afternoon; shall I sign your name on the reserve list? "

" Please — " Alan asked her. He liked a good book now and then, although keeping them overdue robbed plenty of his gold and spoiled true literary enjoyment.

The chitchat continued until she just happened to mention that *Cutting Horse from Wyoming,* starring Spook Hill, the wonder Appaloosa with the college education, was coming to the Granada.

Sure, he had to fumble around a while, but finally he got up the raw brass to ask her to go. He guessed he was the pushy type.

" Oh, I'd love to," she said, acting surprised.

He guessed she hadn't expected him to force her to attend another movie with him, but that was how the big doughnut bounced. Later on, she said she had to hang up because her father was demanding to use the phone for some inconsequential American Bank nonsense. Adults did that to their shy daughters; they butted in all the time.

130

Almost overnight, My Buddy returned to good health and nobody heard a single cough from him.

"I told you it was only a minor cold," Mr. Whitlock remarked at the dinner table a couple of times.

But Alan's mother always replied that it might have been a lot worse without Dr. Bison's wonder drugs in there fighting infection. It proved that being stuck in time saved horses, Alan guessed.

After that life rolled along this smooth freeway of untroubled bliss for maybe two days. Then on Wednesday morning when he was lying around trying to build strength for Condorgas, his mother called him into the living room.

"The mail has just come," she told him. "Here's a letter for you."

She held out one of those envelopes with little windows where the address showed. It said "Alan Whitlock" all right, so he opened it because the thing was probably his.

Inside was a slip of paper with a letterhead printed across the top that read "Karl F. Bison, D.V.S." Farther down somebody had typed "For treating My Buddy, $15.00."

Alan had to read it several times before he got the message; for one thing, it took a while to figure out that Karl F. Bison, D.V.S. was really Lamagra's faithful old man in white when it came to cows and stuff. Then he'd had the logical idea that Dr. Bison thought he'd bought himself a horse, or was making an offer. Finally truth gored in: for driving out here in that beat-up GMC and telling people what Mr. Whitlock, a guy's own dad, had known all along for nothing, the medical profession was trying to gouge him out of all that gold. No wonder Congress and everyone else was screaming! This meant socialized veterinary medicine!

For a second he stood swaying, trying not to swoon dead away from financial shock. There was one last hope and he tried it.

"Mother —" he said, "are you sure this is for me? Couldn't it be for you and Father?"

He let it hang there so she could figure the meaning.

Mrs. Whitlock glanced at the doctor's bill in the same style she read about earth-shaking events in the newspaper — such as collapse of summits and these different wars. One sweep of eyes was enough.

"Oh, my no, Alan," she told him. "This is yours. Don't you remember? You called Dr. Bison to save the life of your poor little horse." She read it some more. "Fifteen dollars! My! That's even more than Dr. Drexine charges for a house call. It must have been the penicillin, dear. Those antibiotics are terribly expensive — especially in such large doses. Remember you said the doctor's syringe held about a quart? That's probably exaggeration, but I suppose a horse does require more than people."

"Naturally — " Alan admitted, his mind jumping ahead to the day when My Buddy caught something serious. "For treating your horse" the bill would read, "ten thousand dollars."

Mrs. Whitlock stared out of the window thoughtfully and toward the neighbor's house. "Mrs. Fegley took Wesley, her Maltese cat, up to Dr. Bison. I believe she said the total bill was either fifty or — Well, a large sum. It was rather unusual for curing a cat, I thought at the time. But I suppose they're as difficult to treat as anyone. More so, because they can't talk and tell the doctor their symptoms."

Alan gasped; he knew that cat. Fifty dollars was forty-nine times too much. He turned away, appalled at the high cost of pet ownership in times of inflation. Pretty soon only people like Rockefeller and the Ford Foundation could own more than, say, goldfish.

Down in the gunk reserves of Condorgas, he was able to face reality. If he paid Bison his fee, something had to give. His wages right now barely bought My Buddy his feed and miscellaneous expenses, with a job of horse-shoeing coming up soon. An extra dollar of debt meant only one thing for Alan: bankruptcy!

132

Reluctantly, he recalled Joe Nunez. "They need pin boys," Joe had mentioned. "Come down and set a few pins, Whitlock. It's good exercise."

Late that afternoon, following Joe's carefully rehearsed instructions, Alan ventured into the Lamagra Bowl and located the manager, Mr. Butch Hawkins, in a dusty little office.

Compared with Mr. Hawkins, No-Pockets Goulart was a great-souled philanthropist who enjoyed knowing sophomores. The guiding thumb of the Lamagra Bowl was shaped like a monster tenpin with a personal bowling ball mounted on top, dominant and rampant. His mien was fat, dark, and ominous with the avoirdupois slipping downward all the time. He implied that he himself had begun life as a born pin boy and from there climbed ever upward in rewarding free enterprise to his current dizzy pinnacle.

"We got a nice recreational environment here," he snarled. "We don't want no pin boys who goof off, see? A kid who wises off and goofs gets it right now, understand?"

Alan did; more, by para-sympathetic reaction he felt the fate of a wise pin boy who let go one goof. Outwardly, though, he described himself as a husky youth who also wished to begin at the bottom of the alley, setting pins, setting pins — if not for the love of it, then for the noble money.

Mr. Hawkins measured this prospect and gave it a whirl. He defined the glittering wage a pin boy took in for setting up a rack. From thence he explained why his alleys hadn't gone for automation like practically every other bowling alley in the country.

It was his love of the youth, according to Mr. Hawkins; the need to stamp out delinquency by keeping a lad's hands and feet busy every evening and far into the night. A Lamagro Bowl Pin setter, he let on, did not have idle hands to do the dirty work. By ten or eleven on a busy night, a Lamagra Bowl pin setter was ready to fall into

133

bed thankful that he was a red-blooded American youth.

Alan felt like saluting, but there wasn't a flag around except for one on a Canadian ad mounted on the wall — and that didn't have Hawaii and Alaska in it, naturally.

"When can you go to work?" Mr. Hawkins sneered, selecting from a box on his desk a fat cigar.

Alan had the impulse to pick up a matchbook lying beside the box, strike one, and do an employer a service. It was a good thing he didn't; Mr. Hawkins didn't light cigars; he ate them. He took a great big chomp out of the one he held and chewed it down. It helped a red-blooded American youth get mature to see a cigar eaten.

" Hours are from seven in the evening on, depending on how many boys show up. We get a big play from businessmen's teams," Hawkins said, chewing some more. He set the uneaten half of the cigar on the edge of his desk with some threads of limp tobacco dangling over in an interesting style. It made a guy realize why Havana was a threat to national security. "When will you start? "

Truthfully, Alan wanted to begin his career as pin boy about one month from next leap year. "R-right away," he fibbed. "That is, d-day after tomorrow." If he could hold off until then, at least he could take Becky to see *Cutting Horse from Wyoming* and have one last fling at being alive before settling down to working at Condorgas by day, and the Lamagra Bowl by night.

" Good! " Mr. Hawkins grunted and ate the other half. " I like a kid who shows up in his working clothes. You begin tonight."

Alan got out of the dim, vast place and breathed air again. Then he set out for home.

For the first time since the Danish cowhand had delivered My Buddy, Alan's resolution wavered. He wondered if that animal had any idea of the kind of sacrifice people all over the country were making to keep his sort of pet.

Now he had to call Becky and tell her he couldn't go to *Cutting Horse* after all. He toyed momentarily with the idea of spinning some fanciful yarn about how he had to be with his horse's delicate health night and day. But if he did, some spy like Leroy Walker would spot him through the smoke of the Lamagra Bowl and tell his woman the truth. Also, among Whitlocks, it wasn't thought good to fib — even to tell white ones for a lifesaving mission such as paying an equine's enormous medical bills.

This probably meant the end of tender romance. It had flowered for a season; now it had to die back, just because a guy's thousand-pound pet got sick. Probably Becky would never get over the slight and the insult.

That night after supper, before he took off for the job, his mother said in a worried voice: "Well, my goodness, Tom. I don't know; I just don't know whether I want Alan to — "

A son noticed there were strange little lights in his dad's eyes. "You told the boy he had to pay the vet's bill, Alice," Mr. Whitlock said like a Supreme Court judge. "Now he's gone out alone and found the employment he needs. It's what a man must do when women remind him of his obligations. I — I admire Alan for his courage."

"Courage?" Dorothea had to chime in. "Him?"

"Yes," replied Mr. Whitlock. "Courage; sustained courage — that's what it takes day after day. You go ahead, Alan. Set pins; sell newspapers on the streets, or — or pencils. Beg if you must, but do anything you can to bring in the — "

"Sell newspapers? Beg!" cried Alan's mother. "Tom Whitlock! Do you realize what you're telling our son?"

After that, his father admitted that selling the *Lamagra Insider* on streets was an exaggeration, and begging around here wasn't too good an idea either. He still insisted that retailing pencils had made Mr. Eberhard a fortune, and that it was these principles he'd been discussing mainly —

the kind that had made America great. If an American found himself with an overgrown horse to support, he claimed, why he whipped in and supported it by hook or book. It was the American way.

When he left for work, Alan had felt pretty good to have a loyal father at his back. Now, amidst the crashing bowls and blasting pins, he didn't know. For one thing, a guy's life was at stake even if he did have this crazy courage. Also an hour of pin-setting was about equal to three of gunking for Condorgas. Maybe it was recreation up at the launching pad of the alley, but down here at the receiving end it was plain hell on earth.

A guy had to keep his eyes on the ball in this game or else; also, he had to keep an eye on each pin, and a pin setter had only so many eyes to go around. That was, he had them now. What he'd have later on was anybody's guess.

Nevertheless, Alan couldn't keep his disobedient mind from wandering. He'd been afraid that romance was dead, but at the same time it meant that gold flipped away on frippery could be stockpiled. Now he was still a little stunned by Becky Linnell's reaction.

Romance wasn't dead; in fact, setting pins had fanned it to this crazy inferno, evidently. When he'd told her truth — that he had to set a mess of pins to pay for My Buddy's medical insurance plan, she'd taken it just the opposite from what he'd supposed she would.

" Why, Alan Whitlock! " Becky had cried out with her girl's voice trembling a little, " I never heard of anything so fine in all my life. You're — you're a true horseman! One of — one of nature's real stablemen, Alan. And we can always go to another movie; we can see *Cutting Horse from Wyoming* on television years from now if we want to."

So here he was in the crashing alleys of horrible life. He had both a horse and a beautiful romance to pay for at the same time. Sooner or later one or the other would have to go, and he suspected which was expendable. A girl had her wily old father to support her, but a horse had —

"Me!" Alan groaned and dodged another flock of pins and the ball in time to save a right leg. For future walking.

11:

Eᴀᴄʜ ᴅᴀʏ now seemed endless for Alan Whitlock, with "gunk that rack and lift that ball" a monotonous refrain. Still, at that, it was surprising how quickly time passed, until he awoke one morning with the Lamagra County Fair and Junior Gymkhana only a couple of weeks distant.

He welcomed its coming because he knew by now that he would never master My Buddy for the simple reason that his equine was a horse genius who mastered people. There was utterly no use telling him anything unless it happened to parallel horse whims of the moment.

Alan earnestly needed to take someone into his confidence — his dad, for example. But it was too late now; he'd gone ahead too long in silence, until he doubted that even Mr. Whitlock would be sympathetic with a lousy horse handler like his son. "You should have told me right away," a guy's dad would say for perfectly logical reasons. "His bad habits are set in by now. A man has to put his brand on a critter while the running iron is hot."

That wasn't exact, but the idea would be the same. Alan had been proud and stubborn; he'd wanted to get My Buddy to like him so that horse would want to do what his owner wished — the way horses did in television and books.

Kind treatment of a high-strung animal, and a lot of soft talk had availed nothing until Alan began to doubt this was really what the authors of horse manuals meant.

138

That was why he no longer dreaded the approaching junior rodeo. It would end this horse farce in a style everybody could understand without a lot of useless yak. There in the ring, with thousands of curious eyes watching, everyone in town would realize that while My Buddy was a perfect horse, no horse could be better than the mind of the guy who rode him.

When they called for the barrel race, My Buddy would decide it was time to demonstrate skill in reining. In musical chairs, he'd start jumping imaginary obstacles. As for general showmanship, Alan knew who'd come in last. He would.

It meant that Becky Linnell would never speak to him again and that Leroy Walker would win her love for aye. But at least that would be definite instead of all this frustrating indecision.

For a while — say, about ten years — people in town would remind him of what an idiot he'd made of a fine horse that day. But in time, guys and women would just chuckle about the old-time humor of it and let a person travel his solitary way. Alan envisioned himself in that future time, pumping Condorgas with his gnarled hands on the fourteen-hour day; then setting pins all night.

"That was Whitlock!" people who dropped in for a couple of gallons or to roll a few frames would remark. "The one without any condor decal or little numbers on him. He serves too! He makes wheels spin in our fair little city."

But he couldn't live on rosy futures. Every morning he had to get up and go resolutely into the gunk-strewn present. Junior Gymkhana madness had infected worthy friends and sound relatives.

For instance, Mr. Hawkins was entering prize chrysanthemums at the Fair; Mr. Fegley had his mind on the Satsuma plum division; Dorothea was grooming King Sinaloa Aztec II for the small-dog competition. She was feeding him rich protein and brushing his coat a dozen

139

times a day besides training him how to stand tall for the judging. Well, if she didn't stop scrubbing him with that brush The King wasn't going to have any coat left to be burnished in glittering sunlight; he'd be stark-naked, and no matter how he stood in front of judges, they'd notice.

Wigwam was entering Xenophon in the natural burro condition. "He enters as is," the guy claimed, "and even that way he's a sure winner. Whitlock, next time try the burro instead of the horse. A burro stands up! "

It was so; a burro was solid and nobody expected one to be a delicate animal all shining with the beauty people expected in nature because most of them didn't have it in themselves. Also a burro didn't need brains; he could stand there being himself and still get blue ribbons.

Right now at seven in the morning Alan whispered to himself, "Next time get a burro! "

He was pitching the hay as usual. The latest half ton of stock was low, he noted. Time to reorder. Also, grain supplies were depleted. With wheat surpluses bursting granaries and upsetting the rat balance while the agricultural problem was upon every lip, Alan couldn't quite figure why it cost a fortune for two sacks of barley.

He'd decided it must be high burlap-weaving costs until his dad told him differently. Burlap was a costly fabric, all right, Mr. Whitlock declared, but the price of the sack was a mere bagatelle compared to the stuff inside. Barley came dear; so did oats. Bran was rough, and the price of alfalfa wasn't exactly hay.

From the nearby stall came the pleasant, soft sounds of a contented horse. Alan glanced in that direction and My Buddy, as if sensing his master's smallest attention, lifted his lovely head above the feedbox and looked through the small open window. He nickered; that horse had a knack for a nicker.

Alan had to grin. "Hi, there," he said with feeling in his warm voice. "Hello, My Buddy! " His tone carried a yearning nostalgia that held a common note with all voices of the growing sophomores in this life who needed a horse to befriend them.

No matter what that equine did, how he acted, or how ornery he became, he had forever captured the heart of Alan Whitlock. Capricious or trustworthy, captious or gentle, the books and movies were certainly right. A horse was noble and beautiful, and the world had lost a true friend and some of its soul when it had turned from the hitching post to the gas pump. The Pony Express wouldn't have been the same if those wiry, clean-spoken, tractable and valiant orphans not over eighteen had made their daring rides in stripped-down Cadillac *coupe-de-villes*. Sure, the mail might have gotten through with less trouble, and Indians could have been stabbed with just car fins but the crazy romance wouldn't have been there. Alan was glad he owned a horse.

At that moment one of the internal-combustion engines that had replaced the horse nagged the flat air, gearing down. The low-slung rod of Newton killed a right into the driveway, kicking a little gravel in cornering, but not much. Alan saw that the front seat was loaded with various heads, arms, and legs, which presently disengaged into the persons of his three pals.

Though they stared right at him while Alan waved a greeting with his pitchfork, one of them — Wigwam — let loose his cry of field and forest. " ALAN! " the guy yodeled. " Where are you at? "

Mrs. Whitlock came rushing out of the back door and said something that produced instantaneous quiet, so in a minute they were coming toward the corral, walking on tiptoe. That was because it was still too early for humans to appreciate Wigwam's rich style of asking whether a pal was near.

" Why didn't you answer? " the guy said peevishly when he was close enough for whispers to penetrate the woodland. " You made me talk out and your mother says neigh-

141

bors are still in bed. Some neighbors you got, Whitlock, complaining all day."

"I did answer," Alan told him. "I even waved this pitchfork."

Tuttle looked surprised. "Oh, was that you, man? I thought somebody had put up one of them mobile scarecrows to protect your precious hay from sparrows. Now that I look, though, a true scarecrow would be a lot more scary."

Newton and Joe Nunez had stopped at the fence and were leaning on it to peer at My Buddy. They talked quietly to each other.

Apparently satisfied with what they saw, both ambled over beside Alan and Wigwam. "Tell him," Joe said. "Newton, let Alan know the style of dirty competition we got now. I can't. Hurts me too much to think." Joe gripped himself to show how thought really agonized a guy.

The tall youth looked down from heights. "Maybe it's Walker's right to do it, Nunez," Chuck said in sweet reasonableness. "It really isn't dirty playing; this is a free country, and horses get born equal too."

That was an angle Alan hadn't considered. A horse got born equal with certain unhalterable rights, and that was why My Buddy —

"It's Leroy," Wigwam bayed like the dire wolf. "Know what that creep has went and did?"

"No."

"No?" Wigwam raised imploring eyes to heaven, asking why. "Well, not only does that rugged, good-looking, intelligent, amiable, lovable, incredible slob own an Austin Healey Sprite, but —"

Joe Nunez moaned with more pain. "Tell Whitlock the rest, Wigwam," he demanded. "Mention about all the women."

Wigwam looked aggrieved. "Was coming to that, Nunez. Nobody can give this here nailed-thumb portrait of Walker without bringing in the women, know that?" He

142

returned to Alan. "You have this passing acquaintance with Walker yourself, chum: rugged, strong, this great athlete who has carried th' Lamagra banner t'dizzy hikes, loaded, as it were, with too much allowance money, too soon? Well, every woman in Lamagra worthy of th' name is mad for the creep. In their private locker rooms, I'm told they sob over a lock of his haircut. But now and then, a stray may stray for a season — like Becky Linnell. They go nutty. Becky's strayed from the guy's futile charm for a while; many do for a few days, but they all come back to Walker eventually."

"Indubitably and inevitably," echoed Newton.

Nunez scuffed his heavy work shoe with reinforced steel toe, which he claimed saved his feet from bowling balls. "Tell him the worst, Tuttle," he prodded. "Don't try to spare his feelings."

"Coming to that, Nunez," said Wigwam somberly. "Don't hurry me none. We've got to fill in Whitlock with the whole story."

"Definitely the full smeller-rayma," Newton put in. "Let him get inside the picture and watch the balloon go up."

"Anyway," Wigwam proceeded, somewhat placated. "Not only does Walker have the cars, the cash, all the women, but besides he's sure to be elected junior class president next year by the conservative vote."

"Namely," added Newton wisely, "those former sophomores who are easily influenced by cars, money, and women. That is, the whole class except for a few individuals who will not be — "

Wigwam ignored him. "Now — " he broke in, "he's gone and done the ultimate. Man, he's run the flag up the crazy old mast. Realizing that for the nonce you had captured the fancy of the one woman we all admire — "

"Becky Linnell — " said Newton and Joe together.

"The Linnell chick," Wigwam amended. "Anyway, realizing her affinity for horseflesh and the Junior Gym-

143

khana bit, not to mention them crazy centauresses, her chums, the Pony Belles, Leroy Walker's gone and bought himself a horse. Whitlock, he's entered all the events. He's got himself out of the bucket seat and into the saddle for this one occasion — "

Alan still held the pitchfork; now he jabbed it savagely into a handy bale of hay. As Newton had said it was a free country — if a guy had the money to exist in it. So if Walker owned a Sprite and everything else, it was logical. To the victor belonged the spoiled, and the more horses the horsier, may the best steed win. That stuff.

"I don't see — "

"I told you, guys," Wigwam screamed. "Told you I knew Whitlock better than he knows himself. I said he'd tell us, 'I don't see why Walker can't own a horse and enter the rodeo if he wants.'"

Newton raised a conciliatory hand. "Calm down, Wigwam," he advised like a statesman. "Don't allow the burro in you to get riled." He faced around. "Alan, you see last night's *Insider?* "

"No," Alan told him. Lately he'd been too tired even to read comics, let alone other news.

Newton fished in his pocket, one of those sewed in a deep-tone T shirt — a Marlon Brando type garment — and dragged out a piece of newsprint. "Read that! " he said, handing it to Alan.

Alan focused eyeballs accustomed to summer vacation. The large letters said: "Casey Elbos, Jim Tibia, Hannibal Walker to officiate at Junior Gymkhana." Underneath in smaller type it read "Many new entries."

He started to hand it back. All a person had to do was read headlines; details came out on television. People said so.

"Read it! " commanded Wigwam. "At least read the last paragraph. They gave that creep a whole section, guys, and everybody else just got his name listed."

Alan read the last part. It said that Leroy Walker, popu-

144

lar son of Mr. and Mrs. J. T. Walker, prominent Lamagra residents, was one of several late entrants. He'd purchased Poco Pronto from the Scalped Indian Breeding Farms of Henryetta, Oklahoma, which was a great horse with bloodlines from Bimbo Dandy, Wooden Cherokee, and Latigo John in his veins. It was one of the best Appaloosa strains ever developed in the Golden West, with enough cow sense to keep a steer guessing all afternoon. The horse had been especially trained at the Lazy Bar-F Training Ranch, and young Walker had entered all events at the local Gymkhana. " I expect to take a first place or two," Leroy was quoted as saying in his modest style. "At least I'll be in there fighting."

Alan handed the paper back without comment. Walker had the right spirit, he had to admit. Everybody else might just as well withdraw now. One interesting sidelight he'd noticed was about the judges. He'd heard of Elbos and Tibia, who weren't much — only the two top point winners last year in the ARA circuit and who were here for the regular rodeo that came two days after the junior job. A calf roper like Elbos and a bronc buster like Tibia got one American Rodeo Association point for every dollar they won in prize money.

" Who's Hannibal Walker, that third judge? " he asked.

Evidently it was a good question. Wigwam let out a shriek of agony and fell against the nearest hay bale. " Told you! " he yelled. " I said, ' Guys, Whitlock is all right but he's pure stupid in some ways ' — " He looked around, brows still knit with pain. " Tell him, Newton."

Newton said: " Mr. Hannibal Walker is Leroy's blood uncle, Alan. He's a rancher in Yakima, Washington. Leroy says his uncle told him about Poco Pronto. Recommended the horse."

Alan didn't reply; no use begrudging Walker a good uncle. Any youth in this age and day needed all the help he could get.

" Don't you com-pre-hend? " Wigwam whispered. " Not

145

only does Leroy have this prize horse from the Scalloped Indian Farm, but he's got the judges fixed. Try, won't you, Whitlock? Think! "

Alan understood, all right. Nearly any judge would be able to pick dead last without too much argument, and a guy could count on a fair shake from the reviewing stand. It was up front where people split hairs, weighed blue ribbons, and fingered the prize money. He didn't need to worry at all.

Even Joe and Chuck were staring at him. Then the tall guy shook his head and laughed. " Shut up, Wigwam," he remarked. " Calm down and give humans a chance. Also stop scaring the squirrels around here."

Joe laughed; he admired Newton a lot.

" As Herbert Spencer once said — " Chuck continued. " But never mind. The trouble with Alan is we haven't given him the evidence a guy needs to use the scientific method. No wonder he's just standing there! He doesn't know about — "

Wigwam moaned. " Was hopin' we could reserve that, but Whitlock's specific density demands. Alan, last night me and Newton were hanging around The Straw Shack, pumping a couple malts — "

Joe said, " We're betting on you, Whitlock! "

Alan looked serious. Whitlocks didn't believe in wagering — especially on a sure last.

" Not exactly," Newton cut in. " We're talking, is all. We want to uphold the honor of — "

" — of us guys," Wigwam finished for him. " You and My Buddy have to win something in that there juvenile go-around. We're clean out on a limbo for you now. We laid our opulent pride on the ice-cream freezer f'rall to see. Walker there, sneering his cooked Kookie style; Becky Linnell there, sneering her calm beauty; and — "

" Becky? "

" With Walker," Wigwam blurted. " They'd just taken in that epic *Ghost Horse of Baywood Park,* and — "

146

Despair surged through Alan. Last night he'd been at the Lamagra Bowl with one ball after another crashing down at him. And where was Becky? At the cinema with Leroy. That hurt.

"Walker got to bragging in his customary unbearable style," Wigwam went on. "Us guys couldn't abide having our sacred honor bescorched that-a-way no longer. So we told him — "

"What?" Alan demanded as the chill grew deeper around his frigid heart. Not only had he lost Becky in order to support a horse, but now —

"That your horse would not only win more events than his, but that if you were entered in the same ones, My Buddy would make Poco Pronto look sick."

"You said that?" in a hushed tone.

"Sure. Us guys are loyal to a pal, Whitlock. We'll stick behind you to the last."

That's where they'd be, Alan knew. Last. But what was done was finished, namely him. Now he had to pick up the threads — like this bundle of pipe threads dropped on your foot.

A while later it developed that his true sophomore companions were here to help train his horse. From now until the Fair, they intended to be here every morning, rain or shine — working out — training — so that My Buddy and his no-good rider got into this hay-trigger condition.

The awful part was that they meant it, starting today. Alan trained right up until the second he had to leave for Condorgas. Wigwam set out simulated objects for the barrel race, pole-bending, and musical chairs, and Alan had to ride the course over and over again. Meanwhile his three handlers sat on the fence and criticized, except when Tuttle howled out "Mike the Spoon" as simulated music.

"Get with your horse more," Wigwam yelled about every ten seconds. "Heels down, toes out! Sit erect! Hold them reins with more nonchay-lance and control! Act like you was born to the saddle! — as if you was part of that there animal!"

Newton was more encouraging and even gave Alan some useful idea, but Joe said nothing.

The strangest part was the performance of My Buddy. He went through the whole routine as smooth as glass, turning now and then toward the gallery on the fence and sort of bobbing his head. He kept his neck arched and lifted his hoofs like a proud dancer.

Afterward, Wigwam said: "We'll be over this afternoon as soon as you get off work. Save something, Whitlock."

"Now wait a second," Alan protested. "I've got to rest because I work nights, too, Tuttle — "

Wigwam waved an impresario's paw in an irritated style. "Makes no difference. You selfish, Whitlock, or are you one of them soft generations the Los Angeles papers like to point at? Won't give up a little time for loyal friends like Newton and Joe? Well, you got to do it!"

In the end Alan had to give in. They were to come back later for another hour of practice and so on until the day of the rodeo. Then they got into the car, ready to take off except that Joe hung back, waiting until the others were out of earshot.

"Whitlock," Nunez said then, "my uncle in San Diego owned horses. I used to ride all the time in Baja, California, with him."

It was a nice thing to know; in every life a horse. Alan nodded and thanked Joe. Right now, My Buddy was back in his stall eating. As for himself, he needed a shower before going to Goulart's.

"I been watching you ride, Alan," Joe said. "Something funny about your horse. It's almost like I seen him before somewhere. I don't mean really; I mean I seen horses just like him with this kind of style that — Well, like being special. Good special, somehow. Also — "

"Sure, Joe," Alan told him. "Well, see you at the bowling alley tonight."

That wasn't exactly a statement of fact. A guy who kept seeing friends at the bowling alley wasn't setting pins according to Hawkins' standards. If he tried to see even one friend for one second, somebody's specially made plastic bowling ball would get him.

But Joe didn't leave even though Newton honked the horn. " Lots of good horsemen in lower California," he said, flashing white teeth. " They know horses by nature, I guess. My uncle says so — "

" So long, Joe," Alan told him.

" I was thinking, Alan," Joe continued, although Newton honked again, " is the chin strap on your bridle plenty tight? Guys in Baja, California, keep their chin straps good and pulled up; not so loose — "

Alan thought that over. The bridle was perfect. " My Buddy wants it that way," he said.

" O.K.," Joe said. " Well, so long. Don't you worry none, Alan."

12:

THE LAMAGRA COUNTY FAIR had always been one of the bright spots for Alan in an otherwise drab year. Like most sophomores, he looked forward to it for several weeks in advance.

The celebration was held annually on permanent ground adjacent to Lamagra Lake, an artificial body of water that featured proliferating cattails, leaky rowboats, and a few bluegill who hadn't wised up yet.

To Alan, the Fair had seemed the epitome of fantastic wonder, especially the midway — one of those touring, dime-snatching compendiums of Ferris wheels, merry-go-rounds, and games of not-a-chance where a lucky citizen might win a two-bit plaster dog or maybe a desicated ham carried from town to town until it was too old to squeal. Local concessionaires, of course, managed the real money-making enterprises, pushing the hot dogs and mustard by the mile and barrel and the sugary soft drinks guaranteed to rot the teeth of even the dentist's kid.

The sunburst of plastic color, the noise, the swelling crowd, and pungent, heady smells all overlaid with a rich coating of honest dust churned by a million feet were memorable still. Yet recently Alan had perceived that the Fair was a great deal more than this outward art.

For one thing, Lamagra County was a place where the Brahman-cross cattle went barefoot whether they liked it or not. Additionally, there were various cash crops like

150

almonds and grapes, hillsides of hay, meadows choked with sheep, pigs, and whole insane herds of turkeys. For some obscure reason, the southern Salinas Valley was thought ideal for those neurotic birds, all breast and white meat and a hundred per cent American.

By now Alan realized that the Fair's true purpose was to sing psalms of praise to one inescapable fact — that Lamagra County had plenty of agriculture. All other novelties and effects were subsidiary but related. There were displays of local art, local talent, and local business, but the heart of the occasion was the big main building where farm equipment and proud town displays of heaped produce told their own story of hard work amidst plenty.

Adjacent to that were the animal pens, a restless collection of bewildered creatures to testify of dilligent husbandry — vast vulgar sows; sleek, square cattle; smug, overheated sheep; rows upon rows of smaller beasts. The year Wigwam had raised game pigs, he had entered one specimen and received an honorable-mention ribbon that carried a cash honorarium of one dollar. Bud Holden was said to have polished three of his mother's windfall Winesap apples, using crankcase oil to achieve high luster, and had taken the sweepstakes in that category.

Yes, the Lamagra County Fair was for everyone. For three hot, dusty, lovely days the crowds milled ceaselessly through the exhibits, sat in the hurting sunlight to witness the Junior Gymkhana and Rodeo and The Roundup, as the regular rodeo was called, and finally they participated in the bidding for fat or prize stock.

It was like a day at an American high school — a good day when teachers were quiescent without opulent ambitions for learning and obedience. Everyone had a fine time and not a little enduring or at least enlightening romance in Lamagra owed its orgin to the festivities.

But this year Alan's expectations had altered; for days he had dreaded the approaching appointment with defeat. So great was his apprehension that more than once

151

he had hoped the calendar would providentially slip a cog like a worn-out missile launching toy and totally eliminate this year's county fair.

Yet he went about preparations with the methodical fatalism of a condemned man. To his astonishment, both Mr. Goulart and the entrepreneur of the Lamagra Bowl were magnificently co-operative — too much so in Alan's opinion. It boded ill.

"Sure you can have that day off," Mr. Goulart had grumbled in his good-natured obnoxious style. "And while you're at the Fair, take a look at our display — "

"Ours?"

"Condorgas!" Mr. Goulart had breathed with an artist's solemn pride. "In the main building. You'll see one of our beautiful plastic condors whirling around in the center." His eyes narrowed as he visualized the loveliness. "All around underneath will be piled stacks of Condoroil in the U-Punch-It supercan. And off to one side — " No-Pockets grew positively lyrical, "will be one of our regular gas pumps, cute as you please. Only instead of real Condorgas, this time she'll pump free KaraKola, the 'wait that inspires.' You know, the health drink. Our company's got a deal with the KaraKola people. It's great advertising for us both."

Mr. Goulart knew all about My Buddy and the undercover challenge. "Just beat young Walker's Poco Pronto," he snarled. "That's all you need to do and I'll say the time you took off is worth making up. Otherwise — "

To Alan the implication was clear. If My Buddy didn't win to further the glory of a Condorgas-connected horse, chances were strong that he'd join the ranks of unemployed shortly.

The message was the same at Lamagra Bowl. "Nunez told me," chewed out Mr. Hawkins. "Claims he'll set his alley and yours too that night." Mr. Hawkins chuckled warmly and ate an especially generous portion of a fresh cigar. "Long as this nag of yours wins, I'm satisfied. Nunez says you're a sure thing to take plenty of firsts."

It was traditional for an entrant to stable his horse at the fairgrounds the night before competition. A guy brought his sleeping bag and slept all night in the aisle beside his steed, sort of to acclimatize both rider and animal to the creepy environment. Not everyone did, of course, especially when the Fair Committee charged plenty of gold for the privilege, board and room for a horse being the inflated consumer item that it was.

Alan's plan was to avoid this and thus postpone the actual moment of his equestrian ignominy. But facts turned out otherwise, largely because faithful handlers disliked half measures.

" You gotta go there the night before," Wigwam insisted. " Us guys don't care if you can't sleep in a strange bed like your own Boy Scout sleeping bag, Whitlock. My Buddy's gotta be there among fellow horses so he can size up the morrow's competition."

Newton was reasonable — which proved a lot worse. " Practically every winner has been on the grounds a full night before the rodeo," he pointed out, producing a homemade form sheet. " I looked up Fair records and talked with some guys. You know Al Woodward up at Carleton? He won three years ago — grand champion in showmanship; all that. Al says he wouldn't dream of not bedding down his horse at the fairgrounds. He says taking a horse right into competition from the trailer is sheer murder, and — "

" Trailer? " Joe Nunez had whistled. " Guys, we haven't thought about that. How do we get My Buddy over there? "

Wigwam looked pained. " That's why Whitlock has to spend the night on the grounds. We don't have no trailer. So we have to ride My Buddy there — across town — through the underpass — all that."

" All four of us don't ride him, naturally," Newton said in a soothing tone. " Whitlock rides him, only even he

153

doesn't really. He leads My Buddy over by hand because some of the way is hard pavement. We don't want our entry to cast a shoe at the last second."

And that was how it finally came about. Despite all of Alan's reluctance and misgivings, the Fair opened on schedule with the usual hoopla and mishap. A merry-go-round proved not so fine when a papier-mâché horse collapsed directly in front of the brass-ring station. Lardo Wibble was the man up on that roan stallion and it had given way at the knees. The concessionaire had publicly denied Lardo's claim that the horse was defective, insisting that Wibble's torso was beyond posted weight limits, and besides, the guy was over twelve in physical age, despite a questionable mental age, and was thus riding under false pretenses. Local gossip said Lardo's folks would sue, but the guy himself was disgruntled only because the gold ring was in the slot right before the accident and he'd missed his sacred heritage to grab it.

Stanley Botts, whose father owned the Purebeef Butchery Shop, had a streak of dart-game luck and won four hams that his dad claimed were still alive. Put a smart pig in the driver's seat, Mr. Botts said, and those hams would walk alone.

The Ferris wheel had gotten stuck for thirty minutes with Margery Mains and Sophia Jensen rumored to be in one car just below George Trotter and Banjo Smith-Wellington. Banjo had loved Margery from afar the whole year past, but sitting there staring at Marge's neck all that time while teetering on high had turned the guy's adoration to hatred, or at least to indifference. Marge had one of these highborn, angry young necks, Banjo insisted afterward.

At last the hour and moment arrived. Newton had loaded the tack box, with saddle, bridle, and so forth, into the car. Then Wigwam and Alan started the long trek across town. Joe, of course, was down at the alley. He

154

claimed he could carry double that way one evening because the cause was just, and triumph he must.

They had waited until darkness had fallen. All evening long, Alan had been getting last-minute instructions from Dorothea, with a few, even from his mother. His dad, though, had said nothing. Once or twice he'd shaken his head a little until a son suspected his father had a premonition about tomorrow's outcome.

Temporarily, night hid them from the public eye, but it was just Alan's luck to be leading My Buddy through the underpass beneath the freeway, with Wigwam behind to watch for traffic and wave it aside from horsefare, when Leroy came tearing along in his spiteful sprite. The little red car was loaded with his own rugged shape, and somebody else.

Walker screeched the car to a halt and peered around in the gloom. " Well, I'm a moneyed uncle! " he exclaimed. " Whitlock! What are you doing there? "

Whatever witty comeback Alan had in head froze when he saw who was with Leroy. Becky! She had that wind-blown, carefree appearance of Western gals who rode around with bronzed types like Walker. So he couldn't say anything at all. Who could?

Wigwam hadn't lost his voice. " Flake off, Walker! " he screamed. " Get out of this here underpass. You'll scare tomorrow's grand prize winner."

" You mean that poor little mistreated nag isn't already scared? " Leroy asked. " Oh, well — Becky — " turning to Alan's former woman, " we'd better get out of here before a truck comes through and floods the horseburger market."

He shot the sprite into gear and snarled away, with the nasty little engine making the underpass echo like a cave.

An hour later, My Buddy and his handlers entered the rear gate of the fairgrounds and at last reached the stables.

Newton was waiting just inside the door. " Where've you been? " he demanded. " And what's this I hear about

155

you trying to thumb a ride in Walker's Sprite? He's been telling everybody that he was willing to give your poor tired horse a lift, but you two guys would deflate his precious tires."

Wigwam made an unpleasant noise. "That's Leroy for you; no sense of humor. Where at is the stall, Newton? You were supposed — "

" It's number 13 down at the far end," Chuck said. " Tell you what: I'll wait here. Be along in a second."

All the way down the aisle, Alan learned Newton's reason. Quite a few entrants in the boys' division were there, some already bedded down to rest nerve and muscle. So they all had something to say about the kind of horse owner who would make his horse walk to the Fair and thumb rides for himself along the route.

"Pay no attention to the multitude," Wigwam told Alan.

It was easy enough to say. Halfway down, somebody hollered, " Becky Linnell thought it was pretty peculiar too, Whitlock! "

Alan's face burned, but he didn't answer because My Buddy was beginning to feel the shame too. He drooped; his head hung low and he let ears sag. His proud master began to hurry until it probably looked as if he were dragging a horse along by rope.

"First prize for showmanship! " somebody else yelped.

Finally they reached stall 13. Alan got clean straw for the floor, a bucket of fresh water, and a little grain. There was a lot of excess whinnying that echoed in the big, spare building, and laughter from guys who hadn't gone to sleep yet.

While Alan inspected the gear in the tack box and laid out his sleeping bag in the aisle, Wigwam had begun to dance around impatiently. " Hurry up, Whitlock! " he kept saying. " We'll miss the Fair. My Buddy's all right now; he's half asleep."

That was true. After a little inspection and thumping

156

around while he got acquainted with the horses on both sides of him, My Buddy had settled down as if he'd been doing this all his life.

Still, Alan didn't feel like going out to the carnival crowd. For one thing, he didn't want to run into Becky again — with her hair that way, and her eyes all lilt and love for Walker. He felt depressed in his mind and heart.

"You go ahead, Wigwam," he said. "Think I'll hit the sack. I — I want to be ready for practice tomorrow."

"Sure," said Tuttle, who was already halfway gone. "Well — be seeing you, Alan. We'll be there in the morning to coach you. Us guys are behind you all the way, know that?"

"Sure," Alan told him wearily. "And thanks."

When Wigwam had gone, he crawled into his sleeping bag fully clothed and in about two hours actually fell asleep. Even so, he could still hear the far-off toy music of the midway in dreams. One comforting thought he had: by this time tomorrow it would be all over and then he could try to forget during the rest of life.

He was awakened by somebody shaking him and opened his eyes.

Nunez! "Hi, Alan," Joe said. "Business was slow so Mr. Hawkins let us pin men off early."

"Great," Alan mumbled.

"I brought you something," Joe told him. "A guy can get hungry in his sleep. Me — I do all the time."

He held a savory sack under Alan's nose. It was one of those foot-long hot dogs with the bun still warm.

Alan's cold heart warmed a degree. It took a real pal to squander pin-setting gold on a foot-long job like this for a friend.

"Also here's one malt in a paper cup — only I dropped a little straw in it on the way down here. You mind a couple real straws?"

Alan smiled wanly. "No," he said. "And thanks."

While he ate with the style of raw hunger a guy builds

157

up in sleep, Joe squatted beside him, watching My Buddy. "He looks real good," Nunez said. " I think he really will win tomorrow. I mean, I've been saying that but not really thinking it. Now I think so."

It was nutty. "Why?" Alan asked sleepily, drinking the last of the malt. Pure straw gave it a neat flavor. Probably all malts should have a shot of natural straw in them. It could start a trend.

"Something about him gives me a kind of hunch. Like I said once, my uncle in San Diego — Well, I can't tell you why, but I got this funny feeling." Joe tapped himself around the stomach. " That's a special-type horse you got, Whitlock."

Alan nodded drowsily as rich, healthful food did its work. He hated to let a neat guy like Joe down but it couldn't be helped. Anyway, every last-place contestant in a meet was always special: the worst. Let Nunez say so if he wanted to.

The day of the Junior Gymkhana and Rodeo dawned with the brilliant California sun. Alan had breakfast on the grounds — coffee and hot cakes served in the main building. Then, with the other participants and the few girls who'd been allowed to spend the night here in the other wing, he saddled My Buddy and headed toward the arena.

The contestants' gate was on the far side and he rode in that direction. Already the morning was bright on the silvery bodies of lavish horse trailers parked here and there along the white fences. To the left of the gate was the judges' and timer's stand, also painted white, with a small spectators' gallery under the same roof for Fair Committee members and town dignitaries such as merchants.

Farther along the fence were the bull pens and the chutes for bronc-riding in the regular rodeo. A little beyond was the barrier for calf-roping and other timed events.

He saw, too, the big horse vans of the Santa Barbara

Mounted Private Eyes — an exclusive riding group — along with the Los Angeles Mounted Sheriff's Posse, which would appear anywhere in the state, no matter how dinky the rodeo. Another fancy rig with gilt trim bore the legend OKIE FALLON'S WORLD FAMOUS SHETLAND PONY FOUR-IN-HANDS.

Alan shaded his eyes and stared across the field toward the big green grandstand where the whole town would sit this afternoon. Even now he could hear the ghostly laughter from the silent rows of concrete seats. "Yea, Whitlock!" he heard the phantom derision. "Get a horse! Either that or get off that one!"

Now, everyone began milling around near the gate, although most of the guys and girls were still dismounted and just waiting. Nobody was on the field yet.

Somebody sighed. "Aren't they wonderful!"

Alan saw what the person meant. It was Okie Fallon's Shetland Ponies pulling two bright miniature rigs painted white, red, and gold. They had been tearing around the track on the inside turn and the judges' stand had obscured the sight from him. The wagons were shaped like small Roman chariots and the two guys driving had these bands around heads and wore short skirts. It was like Ben Hur, only with Shetland Ponies who lived in Oklahoma.

The drivers were cracking long whips over the four-pony teams and the race was pretty exciting. Okie Fallon was here for the regular show, along with Gene McHeel and Oskar Ramage, world famous rodeo clowns who had performed in front of crowned heads on three continents.

Suddenly, Alan wasn't watching the chariot race because he'd seen a more arresting sight. Becky on Miss Moonfire. She wore her Tucson Belle slacks and the whole fancy outfit, with a bright scarf knotted at her lovely throat.

Beside Becky was Leroy Walker tricked out in a pair of Ted Loy sharkskin boots with fancy embroidery, a Mancar Formfit tailored shirt, and a pair of Rusty Ran-

159

cell's West-Kut pants — the best. He was a gorgeous sight, Alan had to admit — particularly to a person in ordinary school pants and sneakers. Not only was Leroy a cinch for next year's class presidency, but he'd probarly win the Nobel prize for high school math and physics as well. He was that kind.

But that creep's vesture wasn't what nailed Alan; it was the guy's horse, this Poco Pronto. That equine stood about a foot taller than any horse on the lot and weighed correspondingly more. He had the perfect blanket and loud markings on hind quarters of the true Appaloosa, while cow sense stuck out on him with more glitter than all the polished metal of his saddle and bridle. On looks alone, every other horse here was licked before the rodeo even began.

"Hi," somebody behind Alan said. He glanced around. Joe!

"Hi. Where are the — "

"Our guys are coming. I got here early." Nunez seemed worried. "Hey, Whitlock, you don't look so good."

"Feel great!" Alan told him. At that he'd slept a full hour. Most of the guys hadn't sacked in that long. He didn't want to take unfair advantage.

"Then what's the trouble?"

Alan pointed. "Walker's horse."

"Yeah-h!" Joe said, whistling a soft note between his teeth. "Lots of speed there for races and stuff. Power too. But don't you worry none, Alan. That horse has got too much cow sense for barrel racing, musical chairs, and stuff. That's a calf-roping horse."

"How do you know?"

"Search me," Joe shrugged. "My uncle down in San Diego — " He trailed off. "I dunno, I guess."

After that they stood there in silence until Okie Fallon had finished practicing and the little four-in-hands came spanking out of the gate, bells jingling and harness flashing. Then all the kids mounted and rode out on the field

160

with Alan and My Buddy dead last in getting through the gate.

Most of the horses and riders headed to the right and bunched up on the far side of the field, leaving an open area in front of the huge empty grandstand. Alan sensed what was coming before it happened and tried to turn his mount toward the rest of the herd, but it was of no use.

My Buddy had taken one look at the cleared area and headed that way. "Please, pal," Alan said to him, "don't do anything now. Wait until we get home and you can practice your event all you like."

From for behind, a horrid voice reached him. Wigwam's. But he didn't look around.

"Whitlock!" Tuttle yelled. "Get over there and practice with the others. Don't take off by yourself. Practice! Get in the crazy swim!"

At that instant My Buddy decided to try the one thing in which he was the undisputed champion of the whole wide world. He jumped an imaginary obstacle. A big one.

Alan had been ready for him and was with his horse, and he had to admit that this was the palomino's finest effort. A record.

13:

THE NEXT few days were going to live in Alan's memory for a long, long time, yet he was never quite able to believe that what happened was real. Even if he could, he'd never know why but there had to be a logical explanation for everything and his dad's idea was as good as anyone's.

He knew, of course, that he'd never been more than a summer horseman and a sunshine rodeo contestant — like most sophomores. Probably people didn't think of that when they got their son a horse, either because they liked the idea or thought he would. Sooner or later though, any guy who wasn't a working rancher had to go through the same trouble and heartache. He pitied whoever did.

My Buddy was gone!

Standing here today with the empty stall and the ghostly corral, Alan still felt a deep sense of loss and a pervasive loneliness. All that remained was the old bridle still hanging there, and one slightly used bale of hay. Left over in uncomfortable abundance was the sadness of a love meant not to be.

A guy just had to face it eventually: horses were out of the romantic past. To own even one saddle horse, a person needed a lot of specialized equipment, unlimited time, and plenty of money. Yet having all these, he still was creating a fantasy whose end result would always be the same.

Sooner or later in every guy's life the past had to go. If its symbol happened to be a horse — a living, breathing

162

animal with a personality — the return to reality tore a big hole in a youth. It was like — like selling out a friend to strangers for money, or — or betraying your own principles. Alan never intended to go through that again as long as he lived because the deed hurt too much. What it did to a horse was anyone's guess.

Right now he thought back to the deadly moment. My Buddy hadn't seemed to mind; he'd lifted his nose above the trailer, whinnied once, and that was it — as if he'd enjoyed the summer vacation with Alan Whitlock and was ready to travel again. Get to work. Maybe a horse could leave a guy without a backward glance. Alan hoped so.

He sighed and continued cleaning the stall. His dad said they could use all this lumber next summer to build a fence around the patio. Mr. Whitlock claimed he was getting tired of old man Fegley staring into the back yard with critical eyeballs. It didn't make for true relaxation.

In a way, My Buddy had gone just in time, because only two days after the Fair, No-Pockets Goulart had fired Alan. So much new business was coming in because of free KaraKola that the Condorgas mentor had decided to put on a full-time man instead of a part-time youth.

Also the job at the Lamagra Bowl had withered. Late summer had turned up as hot as your barbecue pit. People began getting their fun at beach, park, and pool instead of taking recreation in recirculated cigar smoke. With employment spoiled, his horse would have faced either starvation or family subsidy.

From where he leaned on his hoe, he could see the patio. Dorothea came out briefly, followed by King Aztec. His sister was beginning to speak to him again. Only this morning she'd said, "Hello, you awful, awful person!"

The puzzling aspect was that all the wreckage and Gehenna was due to success instead of failure; he'd never before realized that victory could spoil a person's life even more than defeat.

That rodeo! It had been a colorful day, all right, he re-

163

flected, shaking his head in rue. After practicing a couple more jumps, My Buddy had settled down and become willing to practice other stuff. But he'd still been skittish and jumpy.

Once, Becky had ridden close. "What's the matter with My Buddy this morning?" she'd asked.

"He's always this nervous before competition," Alan had explained, hardly able to meet Becky's concerned glance. When a guy's one woman proved faithless by riding around with Leroy Walker it didn't make for easy yak.

"Alan," she'd said abruptly, "I wanted to explain why Leroy and I —"

He never did hear that explanation. Right then, My Buddy had decided to look at the place where the musical chairs event would be run off. And shortly afterward, the handlers and coaches showed up to give advice and encouragement.

"Whitlock!" Wigwam had hollered. "What's going on? Are you daft? I and Newton have been watching your ingenious practice, and maybe they have the events you describe in some rodeos, but not here. Learn to ride a little. Get your crazy message transmitted down them reins!"

Newton said the same thing. "The horse and rider are supposed to go around the barrel on the same side. It looked like you went the off side and My Buddy the near. You're riding the double-barreled race, Alan."

Joe didn't criticize. Instead he stroked My Buddy's neck. "Maybe you should tighten his chin strap some," the guy suggested, but Alan had ignored him. Everything was too tight already.

They'd all gone back to the stable to have lunch. Wigwam disappeared into the livestock exhibition and a few minutes later he'd come tearing back with something blue fluttering from his shirt.

"We won!" he'd hollered. "Xenophon took first in his

164

class. Guys, we got the finest Grade-A blooded burro in Lamagra County."

" There were only two burros entered," Newton pointed out.

" So what? Somebody's got to be second and it might as well have been this sixth-grade kid who owns the other burro. He's young. Someday, us blue-ribbon burro breeders'll have to step down."

Time dragged on while tension mounted. At last the junior rodeo was ready to start and Alan had been glad. It meant that in a couple of hours he could creep home with his crestfallen horse.

The arena looked a lot different in the afternoon. Across the field the stands were full. In the center of the arena a skeleton corps of the Legion band sat on the grass in folding chairs.

In the little tower where the judges sat were three men who all looked alike to Alan — hard-jawed, rugged types with piercing black eyes. The tallest guy, though, hadn't been quite as hard-jawed as the other two who called him Handball.

" Great to have you down with us, Handball," one guy guffawed. " Yeah, Handball," the other bellowed. Alan had recognized the two speakers as Elbos and Tibia; everybody knew them because they were great rodeo performers.

All around, horses and people milled and eddied while across the field people in the grandstand blended their multitudinous voices into a kind of muttering growl — except where an individual let loose his specialized yelp. At the far end of the track, Okie Fallon's Four-in-Hands were waiting, with Okie and his partner both standing at the head of lead ponies to keep teams quiet. Now the Shetlands had worn resplendent gear consisting of bright red-and-gold stable blankets with spangles, and brand-new harness that glittered with brass and colored buttons.

A sort of drum-major's hat brush stood up from each pony's head.

The Legion band had begun to tinker with instruments such as tubas in a disorderly style, one guy having to duck to keep from being clobbered with a careless trombone. Alan had glued his eyes upon them because as soon as they played "The Star-spangled Banner," all contestants were supposed to ride two abreast into the arena, circle the track once, and pull up in front of the stands for an ovation. They'd practiced the act that morning.

A great lassitude had begun to settle over him right there, a sense of overpowering dispiritedness. What, he had to ask himself, did one Junior Gymkhana and Rodeo really amount to in the long sweep of a guy's life? This summer had begun with him barely able to exist; now he was going to end it in the same style. Nothing had changed. What did it matter if My Buddy jumped imaginary obstacles in the musical chairs competition? Did that actually prove anything wrong about the inner horse? The real equine in that steed? No! They would both go on unchanged and unafraid.

Some big-shot Legionnaire came out in front of the band and waved a baton. Suddenly, they blasted out with the music, and people were surprised when they hit the first note fairly well together. The sound threaded to Alan in short brassy gasps while in the stands people started singing. Various Boy Scouts saluted with three fingers except a couple who used two fingers and were possibly still back there in Cub Scout dens. Mentally, that was.

The anthem had ended. Somebody hollered, "Now!" which meant time was ripe for the junior rodeo parade to begin — only there was a pile up of horses trying to figure out which two went in when. Being near the end of the procession made decision easier for Alan and My Buddy. By squinting, he could see that Leroy Walker and Becky Linnell were leading off, that creep carrying a fringed American flag. Becky bore the proud banner of 4-H Clubs of America and it made for a pulse-quaking spectacle.

The whole parade had circled halfway around the track before Alan had begun to notice the change that came over his horse.

That part still puzzled Alan, so much so that here long afterward and cleaning the empty stall he had to shake his head. Why, My Buddy had gotten the parade message from hearing "The Star-spangled Banner," maybe. Near the grandstand, Alan had begun to feel the change just in saddle and to notice that they were staying exactly even with the partner horse, which was Gerald Wibble riding an old chestnut.

Also My Buddy had begun his ballet act, mincing first to one side and then to the other, with his neck arched and his small hoofs dancing.

A breeze had sprung up from somewhere near the mouth of the blast furnace to feather out his white palomino mane while his long, glistening tail fanned back. As they'd passed, people in the stand grew quiet. Somebody howled. "Stay with it, Whitlock. Hang on like a burro."

One of the short races had been the first event, with Alan entered along with about twenty-five other horses. He'd hardly cared enough to catch sight of Walker on Poco Pronto near the center in the best position. He'd heard the starter's gun and felt My Buddy take off, but he really hadn't noticed what was happening until the loud speaker announced the results.

"Poco Pronto, first," the huge, dismal mechanized voice had blasted. "Bonny Boy, second; My Buddy, thir-r-d!"

Right there the crazy miracle of owning a genius horse had begun to happen. My Buddy came in first in the barrel race and musical chairs, second in pole-bending, and third in another race. He'd been holding back his talent the entire time — as a surprise, Alan had guessed. That equine didn't want life to be boring.

Finally, the loud speaker had roared out the wild story: "The show's Grand Prize winner on points —" pausing,

167

"MY BUDDY, the little palomino ridden by — " a longer pause, " A. Whipnok."

So the junior rodeo had gotten finished.

"Congratulations, Whitlock," Leroy Walker had said later on. "Guess that's what it takes to win. A sleeper. Keep a trained, professional rodeo performer like My Buddy under wraps; make him look stupid until the show comes off. That's the style?"

"That's the style," Alan had agreed — only what Walker could never understand or believe was that the guy who'd been fooled the most was My Buddy's rider and owner. One thing sure, he was never going to enter that steed in another rodeo. Next time the result could be the other way around. Maybe next time his horse would decide he was the world's greatest professional rodeo horse-clown, and nothing could stop him from accomplishing any ambition he happened to acquire. Also he'd realized then that falling in Garson's Pond hadn't cured him of a thing, and that he'd probably pretended he couldn't swim just for laughs.

Becky Linnell, too, had ridden by. "Alan Whitlock," she'd told him, her blue eyes snapping dangerously, " I'm never going to understand you. You're — you're a strange boy. But I'm glad you won even though I hate you! I knew you'd win all along."

He'd expected her to despise and loathe him; merely hating a guy was a weak gesture, although it meant the one love of his life was gone forever. A person had to take the bicker with the sweet.

The real shock had come later when Alan was back in the stable getting ready to leave for home the hard way.

Leroy had come by, only this time the man they'd called Handball was with him. "Alan," that rugged drip had proclaimed, "I'd like to introduce my uncle, Mr. Hannibal Walker, from Yakima, Washington."

He'd shaken hands with Handball while Leroy flaked off.

168

"Great performance this little horse and — and you — put on," Leroy's uncle said, his black eyes stabbing this way and that. He moved in and patted My Buddy, looking him over with a fine-toothed paw. "Judges' decision was unanimous," he remarked, "which was unusual. Those professional cowboys are generally a little prejudiced about palominos. Too much Arabian in them for one thing; no speed; no cow sense. Also they don't like a horse who has been bred for nothing but showy looks. They like a horse to win for them. A rodeo performer's horse, you know, does ninety-nine per cent of the work." Handball glanced up. "Of course, this isn't just any palomino, Whitlock. This one is special."

Alan had nodded. How he knew!

"Palominos used to be all the fad," Handball remarked. "Now they're like somebody's double-breasted suit — out of fashion. It'd be hard to get a good price for this little horse in the open market."

Alan agreed; anybody who bought My Buddy would get himself a real equine. That was probably Aunt Ava's trouble; she was out of style.

Suddenly, Mr. Walker had said, "How'd you like to sell this little palomino, Alan?"

He'd refused, naturally, and Leroy's uncle had been willing because he claimed he didn't want to force a boy to get rid of his beloved mount. But just in case Alan changed his mind — especially in view of the premium cash offer he'd made — the man implied he was going to be around town for the rest of the Fair and if somebody changed a mind to give him a call.

About that time, Casey Elbos had strolled up, towing a herd of junior bronc busters and calf ropers in his wake. "Say!" he'd yaked, overhearing the stock-buying conversation, "if you buy that there palomino, Handball, it'll be some joke on ol' Daisy Owens. She still live around Yakima?"

Handball chuckled. "Sure does, Casey! Big as life and

169

twice as horrible. She's got a way with horseflesh, though; that's half the reason I'd like to own My Buddy — because of Daisy. The other half is that my little girl is about ready for a good saddle horse."

One more event had taken place before he'd left the fairground. Leading My Buddy home, Alan had just left the stables when somebody stopped him. Becky again.

"Alan," she'd exclaimed so a guy could tell that her hatred was still blazing inside. "Leroy told me his uncle offered to buy your horse. Is that t-true? "

"Yes," he'd answered. "Why? " When that woman hated a guy, you knew it.

Her lower lip was quivering from pure female rage. " You're n-not going to s-sell that b-beautiful h-horse, are you, Alan? "

"I may — " he'd told her, meaning that people didn't go around giving horses away in this day and age. The day could come after he'd grown old and gotten married, or some other financial hardship had struck without warning.

Well, women didn't use reason; they were pure emotion. Becky had stamped her boot in the dust like a little kid. " If you do, Alan Whitlock," she'd said with more tremulous hate, " I'll never speak to you again as l-long as I l-live! "

Then she'd turned around and run away.

The style she'd been yaking with him lately wasn't too different, he'd thought. So what matter.

That evening, when he'd returned from work at the Lamagra Bowl, he'd found the family up watching television in companionable togetherness, although Dorothea was cross from not getting to go to the Fair again that night. King Aztec II had caught her mood, evidently, and sulked under the set where the big tube kept stuff hot enough for his type of dog.

Alan had told them hello and gone down to his room to think. A couple of minutes later his father rapped on the door and came in. He sat down and stared out of the

170

window a while, which had been odd because it was a moonless night outside.

After a few false starts though, the way most father-son discussions began, Mr. Whitlock had gotten to the point. While Alan had been gone, two people had telephoned: Mr. Hannibal Walker, for one.

" He raised his price a hundred dollars, Alan," Mr. Whitlock said. " He wants to buy My Buddy for personal reasons, he says. He wants to give your poor little horse to his daughter for a birthday present. He owns a big ranch with plenty of pasture, stables, hay — everything a horse would enjoy."

Alan had to gasp when he learned from whom the second call to his father had come. Becky! It was that girl's idea if Alan was really going to sell, that skinflint Linnell would buy the equine and thus keep him in Lamagra.

Then Alan had told his father the whole story about how he'd tried to master My Buddy, the lesson at Garson's Pond, and the style his steed used to maintain the upper hand around the stall.

" What do you think I should do? " he'd finally asked.

" Sell! " his fine old dad had replied instantly. " Strike while the shoe is still nailed to the hoof."

" You mean to Becky's dad? "

" Absolutely not," in a horrified voice. " Sell out of the county. Out of state, if possible! " It turned out that Mr. Whitlock even favored a sale across international lines as best of all, with My Buddy a sort of good-will ambassador to nervous countries behind the rolled-oats curtain.

What really got Alan was that instead of not knowing equines and having this obsessive horse hunger, his dad knew plenty about them. He'd suspected My Buddy's offbeat personality right from the start and consequently had looked into his sales record. That animal had been bought and sold about twenty times in a few short years, having been returned to Happy Meadows Farms alone no less than fourteen round trips.

"What I couldn't understand," Mr. Whitlock continued, "was why he behaved so well whenever Dorothea or your mother rode him."

He'd found the answer. A certain lady named Daisy Owens had trained him as a colt for a rodeo act, but My Buddy hadn't quite been in the circuit's class in her opinion. Besides, fashion had switched to Appaloosas by the time and a palomino wouldn't set off Miss Owens' cool Western beauty the way she wanted. So she'd sold him to some Danes at Happy Meadows, who were probably used to Icelandic horses with fur, but that didn't keep a horse from remembering the precious lessons he'd learned.

"He's like a boy that way," Mr. Whitlock had explained wistfully. "A kid never forgets the red-blooded teachings of grammar school, Alan. I have never forgotten how to subtract by the Greenaway method, for instance, even though it takes twice as long as modern techniques. Miss Greenaway was my fourth-grade teacher. Nor have I forgotten certain poems I had to memorize, or — Well, most of those wonderful three R's. Phonics and the like. It still takes me twice as long to read the newspaper as it does Dorothea."

Alan had to nod agreement; he'd been trained by some fine old teachers like that himself.

"I called your Aunt Ava long distance recently. She agrees. Aunt Ava claims you should sell your horse to somebody like Mr. Walker, who follows the rodeo as a hobby. My Buddy isn't happy unless he's performing; he likes applause and female rodeo queens. He's — he's a grandstander, Alan. You'd be doing him the best favor you could by letting him go back to Yakima."

Alan scraped in the stall with his hoe some more. He sighed. A guy would never forget that day when Handball drove up in the blue car and trailer.

The big man talked a while with Mrs. Whitlock and handed Alan the check. Dorothea was in her room sobbing. But somebody had to stay and watch it so he'd stood

172

alone beside the corral while Mr. Walker led his horse outside.

My Buddy had stepped gracefully along as if he knew all about the climate in the State of Washington. He'd approached the blue ramp of the trailer.

There'd been a lump in Alan's throat and it rose again now — spiny, and as hard as a horseshoe. He'd suddenly hoped that his horse would refuse to get into the trailer, the way he'd rebuked a sophomore so many times this summer.

"Please — " he'd caught himself whispering.

Nothing happened. My Buddy walked right up the ramp without balking or making a false step. He'd stood there eating hay as though he'd been Handball Walker's horse all along.

Leroy's uncle had come back to shake hands. "Got one of those sun roofs for him," he'd said. "He can look out and see what state he's passing through." He'd stared off toward the north a while. "Well, it's a long way to Yakima — " pausing. "Oh, and by the way, son, the next time you own a horse, remember to keep the bridle's chin strap a lot snugger than you had it that day at the rodeo. I still don't know how you controlled this little palomino with a bridle that loose. The bit just pinches a horse's mouth a little. It's the cheekstraps that furnish leverage and let a horse know what you want."

A moment later the trailer had cut out into the street. My Buddy had put his head out of the sun roof and looked back once, and right there Alan thought he'd heard a faint whinny, but he couldn't really be sure.

Well, it proved that a guy who was only a summer horseman should never, never own a horse — at least not one like My Buddy. It took too much gunk to buy the hay for one thing.

Worst of all, it hurt. It hurt terribly in a style you couldn't ever describe, because a horse somehow belonged

173

to the romantic past, and a sophomore human had to live in the here and now whether he wanted to or not.

It hurt a guy!

On that unforgettable morning, Alan Whitlock had turned his face to the corral fence when the trailer vanished from his sight. He choked just once — the dry, soundless sob of a person existing in the urgent necessity of horrible life, a guy who just wanted a little school success, a friendly girl, and a faithful horse.

14:

THE REST of the summer merely droned on in its customary style. There was a week of August weather that shattered all records for heat. Water supplies ran short; sparrows sat around with tongues hanging out and unexplained grass fires kept volunteer fire departments busy almost every day, mostly around two in the afternoon when business got slack.

Alan was restless. Being unemployed and not having a horse to support left him at loose ends, mainly in head. Handball Walker sent a postcard saying that My Buddy had arrived safely and was in good health; his daughter, Sandra, simply loved the horse and he loved her back. Alan guessed equines were fickle that way.

He had plenty of time to regret his own lost love: Becky. Once or twice she let him know how far down the dry well that tender emotion had plunged.

He met her inadvertently one afternoon not long ago. She was standing around in front of Blackwell's Drugstore with some girl chums and it was too late for him to change directions because she'd seen him coming.

From eyeball corners, he noted she was as beautiful as ever, if not more so in her flouncey-douncey cotton dress. Also she was tanned a golden hue a woman gets by horse-back-riding all day in blistering heat, and her hair showed sun streaks. Marcia and Luella were with her, along with other Pony Belles. They were yaking like magpies in their usual charming way — although the few genuine magpies he'd seen weren't even in the competition.

Emerging from the drugstore were a few creamy creeps with big, silly grins on their handsome faces — Leroy Walker and Dan Barry, to take a sampling.

"Hello, girls!" Walker was crying forth and naturally the magpie women looked around. To get a call from Leroy was not to be ignored by any girl; it meant she was one of next year's social leaders in the junior class.

But would Becky Linnell do it? No. She was that style of woman who acted opposite from the normal herd, probably to stir interest in a blasé guy like Walker. She merely stood there glaring right at Alan.

When he was close, she said, "Alan Whitlock, I've been trying to — "

A burst of merry insane girlish laughter from the multitude drowned the rest of her comment.

"Hello, Becky," he answered into the melee, and passed on at a brisk pace. At the magazine rack inside Blackwell's, they even had a sign, No Loitering, and he didn't intend to flaunt the law.

Behind him, somebody said: "Alan Whitlock! You come back here." But that wasn't possible.

The second time was at Lamagra Lake. Some wealthy schoolteacher or librarian had parked his brand-new Sportster Neptune Queen plastic boat at the landing.

Wigwam was with Alan and they were headed down to look at nautical developments. "Yeah," the guy was saying, "had to let my prize burro go, but as my dad says, Xenophon'll be better off."

"Who did you sell him to?" Alan asked, keeping his eyes on the pretty boat. A crowd was gathering.

"Sell?" Wigwam gasped in horror. "Whitlock, you don't never take a pal's full measure, do you? Why, there isn't enough gold in California to buy that dear beast from me. As my dad said, that burro was like a brother to a guy."

176

" Then what? "

Tuttle drew himself up. " I gave him away, pal. To Lardo Wibble's little brother, Junior Wibble. Lardo acted as intermediary in the transaction and I tell you, he drives a hard bargain since he missed that there gold ring at the Fair."

Alan nodded understanding. There was more of a farm situation at Wibble's out on the edge of town. Xenophon would have room to stretch and bray. " Good deal," he'd said.

" Dirty deal, you mean," Wigwam told him. " Lardo is a real Shylark, and you got any gifts for people, don't give to him. He don't count the costs." Tuttle's voice had grown dark with recollection.

" How's that? "

" Know what the guy made me do? I had to give him my blue ribbon. Lardo claimed he needed it as explanation to an innocent kid brother about why he'd brought a burro to the place. He'd only accept him with proof of Xeno-phon's blooded stock."

Before Alan could comment of Lardo's low conduct, Tuttle got a closer view of the Neptune Queen. " Say-y-y," he moaned, " that there's my true boat, Whitlock. Let's talk the lucky owner into giving us a trial cruise."

A guy with Alan's luck should have known better. They pushed through the jostling holiday throng and momentum carried them all the way to the boat even after they'd seen who was at the Sportster's wheel.

The craft was trim and sleek with genuine Neptune fins stuck up high in the rear. A symphony of mahogany deck and streamlining emphasized the Sea King 75 outboard engine, now mute but bespeaking its unholy power even in silence. Any bluegill still alive in Lamagra Lake were destined to know a better way when that propeller got to churning.

The tanned yachtsman sat at her tiller with his captain's hat set rakishly upon the side of his good-looking, rugged

177

head. The guy wore these jet-plane sunglasses, gouged from the native quartz of Abyssinia, probably.

"Hi, chumps," Captain Swashbuckle grinned. He touched a button and the engine howled into life. "Come on, Becky —" lifting his yell above that opulent roar. "Step lively, matey!"

Leroy! who else?

Right there Alan noticed somebody trying to take his elbow along, maybe to a picnic. He looked around and saw a girl struggling to get by so she could jump into Walker's boat.

"Alan Whitlock!" she said, looking at him with frosty eyes, "I suppose you're silly enough to —" The engine roared again, filling ears with good mechanical sound.

It figured; he was silly enough. "Uh huh," he said. "Yeah. Also, pardon me —" He meant for standing in her way.

Then, "Oh, you —" Becky hollered with that positive thinking women could put on. "I — I loathe you, Alan. I think you're the most despicable boy in —" There was more engine noise. A Sea King 75 helped out a lot in conversation, and if a guy had one in school he could probably make U.S. history interesting, even.

Still, that was a lot of territory she'd mentioned in which to hold the championship. He had to nod agreement if she thought he were really meant for the big time.

A pal came to his aid. "Wait a second, Becky," Wigwam yelled, "Whitlock certainly isn't the most despicable guy in — I myself met a slob in Barstow, California, who had it all over Whitlock for plain despicable. And just by stopping for lunch in Los Angeles, you can meet a whole mob of —"

Becky didn't wait; she stepped into the plastic runabout beside Walker and the neat craft pulled out, splattering a cooling spray of surf and sand over spectators. It was a nice gesture. Upon each life a hunk of lake must fall.

Tuttle said, "Hope you noticed how I defended you, pal."

Alan had. "Thanks," he returned, gruffly. "Do the same for you someday." A person needed his friends in there behind him — pushing.

From then on he'd faced the harsh reality that maybe she didn't like him too well. Sure, in future days, he might meet Becky again and they could yak over faded souvenirs. Like in U.S. history next semester; all juniors had to take that subject whether they needed to know historical events or not. Some did; others didn't.

Right now, though, it was plain he had to forget Becky Linnell for aye. She was Leroy Walker's woman, and who could duplicate that geek's pleasing social graces, such as a Sprite, an Appaloosa, and a Sportster Neptune Queen with a Sea King 75? Well, not many.

Stuff like that had made the summer drone. On August 15, he became sixteen years old. His mother baked him a neat cake with sixteen candles that took him three full blows to snuff out. That meant it would be three years before he got his wish — which was to start getting some sleep these warm evenings. It proved how superstition made a person anxious about ordinary life.

There were these great presents a guy got from a family, like a couple of wool sweaters purchased in August sales, a dozen new T shirts, and some slacks for school wear. Also he got a bedspread that somebody with busy fingers had tatted from rags of colorful silks and stuff. It had various college emblems sewed on in its midst, such as M.I.T. and U.S.C. Dorothea had done the work, so he told her that all his life he'd been wanting a good bedspread. For a bed, probably. Not every guy got the birthday spirit smeared on him quite that style. He was lucky.

Then one day Newton showed up in his rod. The lanky guy said he had just quarreled with his woman over a detail. "You," he explained. "You are that detail, Whitlock.

179

Marcia says you're a mean and petty boy-snob of the lowest order. That was the nicest thing."

"Thanks for claiming otherwise, Chuck," Alan remarked.

"Oh, I didn't deny," Newton came back at once. "We battled about forming opinions on hearsay evidence — like hearing it from Becky Linnell. I claim that Marcia should take a good look at you and come to her own conclusions herself."

It would be honest, Alan admitted, but difficult now that Newton was never going to see Marcia again. To help the guy over his broken heart, they began to talk about the opening of school, the dismal event being only two weeks off and looming larger every minute.

In a way, getting back to the grind wouldn't be so bad — with all those inhuman teachers standing over a person full-time and cracking the knout. Getting assigned about a hundred pages of homework every night, plus football practice, would take a guy's mind off troubles.

"Say we have about four hours' gridiron practice," Alan was telling Newton, as he envisioned the bright prospect. "Then we crawl home for about six more on the books. Why, a human in that shape won't even be able to think."

"Sure," Newton agreed. "But what of these endless days now, Whitlock? What'll we do until then? We have to think; we can't help ourselves with these brains we've got. They think whether we want them to or not."

It was true and they might have done some thinking then and there if Joe Nunez coming by in his old cement-mixing car hadn't saved them.

Joe got out and handed Alan an envelope. "Here," he said. "Happy birthday, Alan. It's a few days late but I just remembered from last summer when you had a party. Good cake then."

It was a birthday card that had some rosebuds embossed upon it and read "Happy Birthday to a Dear Friend."

The next day Newton was over early. "Got to thinking

when Joe brought his card, Alan. How old are you? Sixteen? "

Maybe he looked younger, Alan guessed. " Yeah," he said. " Why? "

In the next couple of minutes Newton unfolded his plan. As a new type birthday present, he wanted to take Alan up to Paso Verde, where the California Highway Patrol hid out, and help a pal take the test for a driver's license. " You could surprise your folks that way," Chuck suggested.

They did just that and Alan passed the written part with only one mistake, which was about overtaking a school bus. It was his idea that a driver shouldn't overtake a school bus at all. If he saw one, drive up another street. Some of the bus drivers they had could take down a guy's number for breathing too fast at the wheel.

The driving examiner they had was a civilian. Alan sized him up immediately because he had the same thin eyelids and arched neck as My Buddy; also he was equally skittish, if not more so.

As they drove around in Newton's car, making stops, parking, turning left whenever the guy said to do it, he was as careful as he might have been when riding that horse. No use to startle something with thin eyelids like that, so he drove smoothly, not taking chances or trying to cut in even when it would be a good lesson.

Finally, he eased up in front of the CHP office at about two miles an hour and stopped. The examiner got out and stood swaying in the breeze while he marked the sheet on his clip board. " I've given you a good score, Whitlock," he said. " For a teen-ager you drive almost carefully. It was a pleasant surprise."

Alan got the license.

" Now use a little psychology," Newton advised. " Leave it around home on the living room table and places. No telling what may happen."

Although it was futile, Alan tried it. Surprisingly enough

he got some results. One Friday night his dad came down to his room.

"Alan," Mr. Whitlock said, "how would you like a car of your own to drive this next year?"

Alan was astonished to learn that he had his own money to buy one. He had forgotten about Handball's check because it had seemed like blood money at the time. After a while, his dad was able to convince him that My Buddy wouldn't object to some of his purchase price being spent on an automobile. That way, he was a modern horse.

On Saturday they went to San Luis. Alan's father drove directly to a used-car lot on the far side of town. Getting out, he walked straight through a whole mess of shiny fin and tin to one job sitting near the back.

"Now this is a car somewhat along the lines you might want as a beginning automobile," Mr. Whitlock said.

It showed what kind of luck a businessman enjoyed. The first rod he touched turned out to be the best, whereas a sophomore could search for a week and still get hooked. It was a sedan, but it had a rebuilt short block and new paint. The running gear was smooth, with a nearly new set of brand tires.

Alan bought it, although his hand trembled when he signed the contract.

Another indication of Mr. Whitlock's facile skill in commerce was the insurance policy that he'd already bought from his own company merely by chance. This day and age, everybody had to be insured. That way, if some idiot plowed you, a guy's mangled fenders got straightened out by the company's benevolence.

Since it was the style to name a rod, Wigwam suggested calling the car "The Black Window," claiming Alan could paint one black as a symbol, even though the finish was a sort of robin's-egg blue. But none of the names Alan could think of seemed appropriate. Later on, he figured, the right idea would come to him.

And so that summer ended at last, with good and bad

182

each a part of it. Maybe that was how life went on, with these crazy hills and valleys.

Worst of all, he had lost My Buddy. A guy could never forget him when the ghostly wild horses of eternal boyhood took a notion to go galloping through. Also he'd lost the love of Becky Linnell.

But as he dragged town in the legal style of a true Whitlock — lonesome and alert — he could forget a little. The muted mellow rumble of his tail pipes helped drive away the melancholy of a love too young to exist.

It went on that way until the day finally came when school took up again. A proud junior had to shoulder the burden.

Of course, Alan awoke that morning with the old weary reluctance, sure. Who didn't? Yet in a morose style he was glad to climb back into harness. Being a junior was a large deal around Lamagra, and a guy still bowed with drear sophomore days wanted to get up there into the hollowed old halls and grab some living.

There was the prom ahead, and — well, a host of stuff that needed a guy's attention.

He wasn't surprised to run into the same old pile up about who was in the bathroom when. Life. Also his mother was there in the kitchen as of old, making people heap in a little more food for energy. More life! In a way, living was merely another stack of hot cakes with maple sirup, another glass of fresh orange juice, a few plates of scrambled eggs. Nothing more; nothing genuine to go on. Fantasy.

As usual, Dorothea was screeching her head off because this was the only freshman year she'd ever have for big experience in girlhood. Yet Alan noticed a trifle less steam behind her style when she spoke to a brother who was a junior. She even asked a couple of sensible questions about education, such as, " Where is the awful office, Alan? "

" Want to ride up there with me, 'Thea? " he asked in a burst of philanthropy he'd likely regret.

183

But no; Dorothea preferred walking with Suzie Frazier and MayBelle Claasen. They wanted to sweep into the halls and dazzle callow youths still confused by a new environment. Alan knew; he'd been a baffled freshman once himself. The chums arrived and his sister took off with them amid King Aztec's hysterical *alohas*.

"And don't you worry, Mother," he said when it was time for him to leave. "I'll keep up my grades. A car won't make a bit of difference with the kind of grades those teachers will give me."

For an instant before he started the engine, he passed his hands over the smooth wheel with that pride of ownership a guy gets in his own rod. This year was going to be different, he guessed, because he was really with it at last — a Californian on a set of shimmering wheels with ripple hub caps, rolling along the broad freeways of America.

The last thing he saw as he dug out was that lonely fence on the hill with the empty stall. It had been a great summer, but now he was leaving it behind him and in doing so, Alan Whitlock sensed that he was driving away from his own boyhood at last.

The morning was perfect, cooler than most here lately, with the trees dusty green and the sky blue as space. Yes, it was hard work to live and be sixteen — with all this hoke and poke of high school up ahead that adults thought was good for a guy. But being alive was the best style of living he'd run into yet, so why not stick around?

He glanced back once toward the corral, almost as if he expected My Buddy to be there seeing him away to the cement tents of learning. But of course that equine was up in Yakima with Handball. Alan hoped he was free and happy as a horse.

He began to see guys and girls on their way to school in colorful garb, singly, or in knots and bunches, walking, or riding in cars or on bicycles. The American way!

Abruptly, he killed a right up Ridgewood Terrace toward San Jacinto. It was a better route, farther but

184

smoother. No use to wear out springs.

Then he eased back with the alert nonchalance of an old pro of the road while he listened to the engine with a practiced ear. The rod had a mill all right — smooth, quiet, holding back the power to a person's slightest calibration with the accelerator, but ready with the most if need be. In this modern age, if an automobile jumped an imaginary obstacle it would put too much suspense into daily traffic.

He percolated slowly beside a tree-shaded walk where the morning sun cast feathery shadows up the hillside above. By merest chance, he happened to spot these three women strolling together and it hit Alan that he could be acquainted with them. One had russet hair, for example.

He decided to let them walk to school because hiking was good exercise for women. It put the old bounce in their step and brought good health creaming to their apple cheeks. People in Europe did a lot of hiking and bicycle riding for fun.

Yet as he came up beside them, an impulse hit him. His foot eased down the brake as the car came to a smooth stop. He noticed that the women came to a stop too.

"It's Alan," a magpie chattered, one that sounded a lot like Marcia James. She made him think of the raven in Poe's poem he'd read as a freshman.

Well, a junior had to dig up the courage to look the world square in the teeth — especially if he intended to drive a car places and bring it back alive. And what were women except a normal part of almost any geographical location like Lamagra? Nothing. Also you were supposed to give a neighbor a lift; people even said so.

"Like to ride up to school?" he asked.

There was a brief whispering debate among the three.

"We'd love to," the woman with russet hair said. "Alan, what a nice little car this is. There's room for all of us. It's not a bit like one of those silly little Snipes where only two people can be comfortable."

He knew what she meant. They'd all get in the back

185

seat and let him taxi them up to school in their customary highborn style. But what did it matter, really? When a guy's love was lost, it was gone, man.

"Thanks," he said, deep-tone, as he opened the door. "Hop in." Then he turned away and stared across the wheel toward the open road. Let them get in any way they wanted; he didn't care. The car door slammed and springs gave. These days a few women really loaded a rod to the axles. They weren't the same frail, wispy flowers that horses had lugged around in bygone years. Maybe the automobile had come just in time.

"All set?" he asked.

"Yes," somebody said from the seat beside him.

At first a chill electrocuted a spine, but he regained poise. So two got in back and one in front! So what did that matter in the long pull ahead? Let each woman who would ride choose a place. He shot the car into gear and dug out of there, gently, but with firm determination.

After about a block he began to consider a driver's obligation to passengers. A guy ought to know which ones were where, actually. That way he could look to individual comfort.

There was a clear space of straight road ahead. Within, he turned and did a lightning take of the girl beside him, returning eyeballs to the way ahead instantly. Good drivers didn't let attention wander. Not for very long, at least. They didn't stare at objects beyond their regular periphery of driving vision.

"Hi, Alan," an object said.

There was this small silence — except, of course, for the endless back-seat yak — school, clothes, boys, teachers, sports; details. Slowly a kind of warmth penetrated the chill obelisk of Alan's heart. He'd learned about life this summer; now he knew a secret about girls. That is, about a certain girl.

Sure, she hated him; their love had died hard this summer because of cruelty to a horse. But maybe a woman

186

could hate a guy for the horse side of him, and like him because he had a mechanical mind. During the junior year ahead, Becky's loathing of him might thaw a little, he figured. That was, if he played it right.

He tried out several replies in head — the gay wit of Leroy Walker, Wigwam's wisdom, and Newton's crazy poetry. None of them seemed to fit the occasion.

" Hi, Becky! " he said at last, deep in his throat.

Nothing more. For one thing, he couldn't get the suave chitchat to flow farther, and besides, up ahead was Lamagra Union High School. Around that kind of traffic, a guy had to keep his hands on the wheel and his mind on the road the whole time. No lie.

BIOGRAPHY OF JAMES L. SUMMERS

JAMES L. SUMMERS was born in Oshkosh, Wisconsin. When he was a child his family traveled a great deal so that he went to school in Wisconsin, Indiana, Illinois, England, Germany, Connecticut, Cuba, Hawaii, Oregon, and finally Arizona where he graduated from elementary school. After graduating from high school in Milwaukee, Wisconsin, he spent a year in foot-loose travel, in Canada and the United States, and went to sea from Brooklyn as an engine wiper. He visited the West Indies and other ports and finally returned to school at Chaffey Junior College in California. After a year there he matriculated at the University of Wisconsin but his college days were cut short by illness.

The following year he attended summer session at the University of Southern California where he met the girl who was to become his wife. They were married the next winter while Mr. Summers was a student at the University of California at Los Angeles. During the depression Mr. Summers had to leave school and he worked at many jobs; he was a vacuum-cleaner salesman, a neon light repairman, a truck driver, and eventually owner of a small electrical business.

Still wanting to finish college, Mr. Summers got a night job, and after two years received his A.B. degree at U.C.L.A. He then started teaching. Writing interested him also, but it was a few years before he sold any stories to the national magazines. One day an editor sold a story for him to *Seventeen* magazine, and from then on he wrote almost exclusively for young people. Now Mr. Summers is writing novels for teen-agers and young adults. His story *Girl Trouble* was selected as an Honor Book by the *New York Herald Tribune's* Spring Book Festival Committee. *Prom Trouble* was a Junior Literary Guild selection and *Ring Around Her Finger* was a selection of the Young People's Division of the Literary Guild. Mr. Summers lives in Atascadero, California, and has retired from teaching to make writing a full-time career.

C1